The Perfect Pretext

William M. Johnson

Best Wishes

Will

PublishAmerica
Baltimore

This is a work of fiction. The characters, incidents and dialogues
are products of the author's imagination. Any similarity to actual
persons, places or events in purely coincidental.

First printing

ISBN: 1-4137-8500-X
PUBLISHED BY PUBLISHAMERICA, LLLP
www.publishamerica.com
Baltimore

Printed in the United States of America

Preface

Seen from a spy's perspective, "the perfect pretext" has the following characteristics:

* It can be used by men and women of all ages. Intelligence officers use this pretext. So do private investigators, competitive intelligence agents and amateur spies with their own agendas. No special attributes or physical characteristics are required.

* Language is usually not a problem. The pretext is based on a legitimate activity enjoyed by millions of men and women throughout the world. Their shared interests bridge most language barriers.

* The perfect pretext can be used any hour of the day or night, and can be adjusted to fit most weather conditions.

* This pretext fits any terrain and almost any location. It can be used on a grassy hillside overlooking an office park, on the roof of a high-rise building in the business district, or on a boat in the bay near the docks.

* The perfect pretext provides a logical reason for having binoculars, night scopes, camera equipment, listening devices and recorders at the pretext site. In fact, the pretext would be less credible without at least some of this high-tech equipment.

* Reputable organizations in many countries unknowingly support this pretext, though ID cards and official credentials are not required. Many legitimate groups and organizations issue membership cards and sell specialized books and other merchandise used by spies in this pretext.

Birding—bird watching—is the perfect pretext. Birders watch birds. Spies use birding as a pretext.

Q-42, What is the perfect pretext? From the book, *101 Questions & Answers About Business Espionage*, by William M. Johnson, ISBN: 0-916775-02-X, (Nonfiction).

Chapters

Chapter 1
Falcons on the 14th Floor

Our value systems are the guideposts of our lives. They determine who we are, how we relate to the world around us, and what we will become as our life progresses. They define us in ways that words alone cannot, since what we say is far less important than what we do.

Adrian Warren stood on the ledge outside the window of the women's washroom on the fourteenth floor of the financial center, looking out on a foggy night. His value systems were those of a charming, immature eighteen-year-old thief who thought that rules were made for other people. His value systems had been developed as a by-product of an undisciplined childhood and an education that was a yard wide and an inch deep. His guideposts were faulty, and had led him astray.

This was the last night of his life.

The women's washroom had the only window that opened on the fourteenth floor, a last concession to the ornate marble and cut-glass elegance once evident throughout the financial center, but lost during the last remodel. The mirrored and marbled women's washroom was one of a kind, and had once been featured in the lifestyle section of the local paper.

The night smells on the ledge outside the washroom window were a mixture of expensive perfume, bird droppings, wet masonry and the soft dove-gray fog of the spring season. Adrian took a deep, wet breath of Northwest weather, and began to work his way along the ledge. He was there to steal *eyasses*, young peregrine falcons still in the nest. He wore blue janitor's coveralls, and carried an empty drawstring bag to carry the falcon chicks.

A pair of peregrines nested in the gravel of a shallow box on the ledge on the east side of the building. The nest box was provided by the city birds research project, and was sponsored by a local attorney, Irving Cordell.

The female falcon laid four eggs in the gravel of the nest box the last week of March. The nest in the gravel was called a *scrape*, the nest site an *eyrie*. The eggs hatched within a forty-eight-hour period, synchronous hatching after thirty-three days of incubation. The young were being well-fed on several types of small birds, headless and plucked, along with torn pieces of city pigeons. Eyasses fledge forty-two to forty-five days after hatching. The smaller males, tiercels, developed faster, and usually fledge first.

Adrian had followed the progress of the young birds on the City Birds website, and decided to steal the eyasses before they fledged. He had entered the financial center prior to closing, hidden in a cramped storage area that had been his domain during a brief summer job, and now moved slowly as he felt his way along the ledge. He wasn't afraid of heights, but the fog made the ledge slippery, and a penlight stuck in the hatband of his hat did not provide much light. He had seen this penlight technique used in spy movies on television, but found that it didn't work very well in real life.

As he felt his way along the ledge, he heard what he thought were the soft sounds of ropes and pulleys behind him, a presence he felt rather than saw, because of the fog. Yes, he was sure, ropes and pulleys. He had watched the window washers go up and down on their staging when he worked in the building, but who would wash windows at night? He heard the staging stop, then bump gently against the building as someone stepped from the swinging platform onto the ledge. He realized he wasn't alone. There was someone else on the ledge behind him, between him and the women's washroom window!

Adrian stood still, almost afraid to breathe, as a man in dark-colored coveralls went in the window of the women's washroom. He could see the man briefly silhouetted in the dim light from the window, but couldn't distinguish his features.

Adrian's legs began to shake, and the ledge beneath his feet seemed suddenly less solid. He hadn't felt the height before, but now felt it in his bones. His only escape route was back through the women's washroom window, and it was a long way down to the street below. He abandoned his plans to steal chicks, and just wanted to go home.

He waited a few minutes, then moved to the window to see where the man had gone. He looked in the window just as the man in the dark coveralls retrieved what looked like videotapes from the ceiling of the janitor's closet near the washroom door. His refection in the beveled mirrors above the sinks bounced back and forth as multiple images.

Adrian recognized Ramsey, the private investigator who did volunteer work with the city birds research project, but that didn't make him feel any better. He'd met Ramsey while working in the building during the summer, and had always felt intimidated. Ramsey was big, stood too close to you when he talked, poked you in the chest with his forefinger to make a point during one-sided conversations, and pointed and cocked his forefinger like a pistol when he passed you in the hallways. Ramsey was just as intimidating during Spy School at the zoo, which was one of the reasons Adrian had quit going to class.

Ramsey put the tapes in his coverall pockets, and then came back out the washroom window, the way he went in.

Adrian moved away from the window to hide in the fog-shrouded shadows along the ledge, but had forgotten that the penlight stuck in his hatband was still turned on.

Ramsey saw the pinpoint of light just as he was about to step onto the window washers's staging to go back to the roof.

Ramsey worked for attorney Irving Cordell, one of the sponsors of the city birds research project. Ramsey used birding as cover. This gave him official access to several downtown office buildings, including the financial center. He helped the ornithologists rig the window cleaners's staging they used to chart the progress of the falcon chicks on the ledge on the fourteenth floor, then used the staging for his own purposes when they weren't around.

Ramsey had obtained access to some parts of the financial center by bribing one of the security guards, but many of the newly remodeled private offices were now protected by modern burglar alarms. These systems used biometrics and other sophisticated identification systems that logged people in and out of the offices by date and time. They were difficult to defeat without alerting someone, either during the attack or after the attempt.

As a spy, the best way to bypass these sophisticated burglar alarms was by coming down the outside of the building to plant the audio/video bugs that were basic to his business. He used a wide range of technical surveillance equipment, including wireless pinhole cameras and transmitters.

Ramsey used a cordless drill to make small holes in the window casings of the boardrooms and private offices of his targets. He also bugged the furniture storerooms where sexual adventurers met to live out their fantasies on the ornate davenports, love seats, and overstuffed chairs left over from the last remodel. Everything the audio/video bugs picked up was transmitted automatically to the receivers and recorders at his listening post in the ceiling of the janitor's closet. All he had to do was stop by from time to time to pick up the tapes.

The tapes went to his employer, but Ramsey made extra copies of the intimate pictures of women, what he called "chick pics," for his own collection. He refocused and enhanced the sexual features of the women, and played the tapes over and over for his own enjoyment.

Ramsey had just replaced the batteries in one of the older units. The batteries were always the weak point, but running power cords from inside the building to power the various audio/video devices would have been pushing his luck.

Ramsey saw the pinpoint of light in the shadows along the ledge when he climbed back out the window. He reached inside his coveralls for his pistol, then recognized Adrian as he turned in his direction and the fog reflected the light from the penlight in Adrian's hatband back in his face. It was that kid from Spy School, though he didn't often show up for class. The kid was a spy wannabe who had read the book, The Falcon And The Snowman, and fancied himself a falconer. Ramsey thought he was more like one of the city pigeons. That was the way of the world, especially in the city. You were either a falcon or falcon food, and the kid was a born loser. He didn't need a pistol to handle a loser.

Ramsey knew who Adrian was, and guessed why he was there, but he wasn't sure how much the kid knew, or if he had seen the tapes. He had to find out.

"Hey kid, what the hell are you doing here?"

Adrian couldn't think of a believable lie on such short notice, so he did what usually worked well with his grandmother, Maggie. He told part of the truth, the part he hoped wouldn't get him in trouble.

"I'm scouting chicks. So what? Isn't that what you're doing?"

Ramsey thought of his private collection of pictures taken in the women's washroom. "Yeah, kid, you could say I'm scouting chicks."

Ramsey could see that Adrian was nervous. Was it just the height, being out on a ledge on the fourteenth floor at night in the fog? Or was there something more? He had to know for sure. The kid had seemed like a simple shit the few times he turned up at Spy School, so a simple bluff should work.

"So, kid, I saw you looking in the washroom window. What did you see?"

"I didn't see anything."

Ramsey moved closer. "Don't lie to me. I'll know if you're lying!"

Adrian was scared, but again, he couldn't think of a believable lie on such short notice, so he told a half-truth.

"You were taking some stuff from the janitor's closet. I don't know what, and I don't care. Besides, it's none of my business if you steal stuff from the building."

Ramsey wasn't buying it. If the kid had seen him taking something from the janitor's closet, he must have seen the tapes, and perhaps the equipment in the ceiling. No question about it, the kid had to go. He would make it quick, go back up to the roof on the staging, and be gone in a few minutes. No point in putting it off.

"Are you a Jew?"

Adrian had a funny coppery taste in his mouth.

"No, I'm Catholic."

"A Papist? That's just as bad. It's always easier when the pigeon is one of the mud people, or a Jew, or a Papist. You all deserve what you get, one way or another."

Ramsey stepped onto the window washers's staging, then moved the staging along the ledge. Like most young men, Adrian had never visualized his own death, at least not one that wasn't heroic. He moved as fast as he could along the ledge, but Ramsey moved faster.

Adrian tried to shout as Ramsey swung the staging toward him, but the sound that came out was more like the croak of a city crow.

"You can't get away with this! Everyone at Spy School knows who you are. Maggie will kill you! She's done it before!"

Ramsey hit him with the edge of the staging. Adrian's fear changed to anger as he felt his ribs crack from the impact, and then went over the side. This was all wrong. *Death wasn't supposed to happen like this!*

As fate would have it, he didn't fall far, but the fall was final.

Chapter 2
The Indagator

Ian Scott arrived at the zoo an hour early to teach the evening class, the class the students called "Spy School." The correct title of the class was "Wildlife Surveillance with Camera & Recorder," but as someone had pointed out, the birds hadn't given permission, or signed a release, so birding was actually spying.

Arriving early for appointments was a habit he had picked up from years of working as a counterintelligence officer in foreign countries where checking out his surroundings before a meeting was always a good idea. He was now back home in the States, but habits are hard to break, and the world was still a dangerous place.

He sat on one of the benches near the zoo entrance and massaged his sore ankle. He wasn't that old, but found himself sitting there in the evening sun like some old pensioner trying to make sense of his life, and wondering how he had come to this. He was divorced, had no family, not even a permanent home. He was working part-time for his former employers, and was lucky to get even that. Most people would say it wasn't much of a life.

Ian put his foot up on the bench to tighten the laces on his left shoe. He had a sore foot, an old injury which caused a slight limp when he walked if he didn't give the foot extra support, especially when he was tired. The limp was a constant reminder of a painful episode early in his government career, an incident that he had never been able to live down.

He winced as he tightened the laces. He lived in the present, and wasn't someone who spent time contemplating his navel, but it was difficult not to think of the past sitting in the sun on a park bench, massaging the sore ankle that tied the past to the present.

Pain was a powerful reminder. The past came flooding back.

He had been on duty as a security officer with the consulate in Frankfurt at the time of the incident, but the circumstances had been less than heroic. He not only hadn't saved the day through some brave act in the line of duty, he had barely been able to save himself. He had taken a lot of kidding about it over the years, a standing joke that began with the question, "How's your foot?" and ended with a grin, and sometimes with muffled laughter. People don't forget a sex scandal, especially when most of the juicy details are known and are part of the official record.

It had begun well enough, with a promotion. He had been the new boy on the block at the consulate, someone to periodically pull the cores and change the settings on the less critical locks, and perform other mundane chores while waiting for his status to be upgraded. While he toiled as a glorified housekeeper, the powers that were (he never knew who to blame) sent him down to the basement for orientation with one of the technical surveillance countermeasures people, one of the good old boys, one of the ancients.

The TSCM man told Ian he used the initials W.P., but didn't say what the initials stood for. Consulate wags said they stood for "wires & pliers." W.P. was a fat little man who had, according to rumors, spent too much time sitting too close to his test equipment, including the signal generator. He was good at his job, but considered a bit eccentric. His hobby was robotic eavesdropping—robot bugs—and he sometimes talked to his tiny creepy-crawly creations while he worked on them. A father talking to his electronic children, who sometimes talked back. Ian hadn't known this at the time, of course.

W.P. began the orientation with an overview of audio/video eavesdropping, then outlined some of the basic countermeasures he employed while doing electronic sweeps, his primary job assignment. He spoke at length about "electronic sophistication," and made it clear that Ian and the other security officers without his specialized training were amateurs sent to him primarily to learn what *not* to do, so as not to get in his way. W.P. believed in SIGINT, Signals Intelligence, the way a religious fanatic believes his version of the truth to the exclusion of all others, and thought HUMINT, Human-source Intelligence, gathered by agents and informants, was dangerous and overrated. He used the word, "asinine," several times; it was obviously one of his favorites.

When W.P. saw that this part of the orientation wasn't going over well—Ian was getting red in the face—he became conciliatory. "Don't take this personally, Ian. We're in this together. We're both indagators, hunters circling game."

"I don't know what you're talking about."

W.P. laughed. "That's life. This morning you didn't know what an indagator was, this afternoon you are one." He leaned back in his chair and put his feet up on an empty equipment box. Ian made do with a stool at the cluttered workbench.

Ian could see he was in for a lecture, something to be expected when one of the good old boys had a captive audience. Technical people who worked behind the scenes were often lonely, then talked too much when they got the chance. W.P. was apparently most eloquent when faced with a new target.

He said, "Indagators love the thrill of the hunt. Man the tracker, the hunter, the indagator. Catching spies is the hunt at its most exciting. Man the hunter, also being hunted. Once you get hooked, no other career will hold your interest, at least not for long. You'll see. It'll happen to you, if you last long enough."

Ian doubted that this was part of the official orientation, but W.P. wanted to talk so he smiled and nodded. Electronic debugging was labor intensive, and probably boring. W.P. spent most of his time poking around in basements, crawlways and janitor's closets while loaded with test equipment. One of the sweaty counterintelligence arts, at best. Let the old boy talk.

W.P. said, "I was hooked the first time I found a bug, back in 1984. The one in the headliner of the Ambassador's limo. We thought it was planted by one of the office interns at first; he was banging a local girl in the limo after hours, and we knew he liked to record his conquests. It wasn't him. The guy who did it was actually one of the locals who worked in the garage. Of course, back then spies didn't have all the high-tech stuff we have today. I remember..."

Ian had heard the story before, though the date, the place and the sexual positions assumed by the players had changed with each telling. Paris in 1990, London in 2002, front seat, back seat, jump seat—the story kept being updated.

W.P. was off and running, one story leading to another. It was only a matter of time before the phrase, "I really can't talk about it, but...," carried W.P. to the realm of myths and legends. He was telling war stories the way so many of the old spooks did, by scrambling names, dates and places. Ian listened for a while, but soon got lost in the scramble. He had already heard variations of most of the stories while enrolled in the protocol course for attaches at Bolling Air Force Base.

W.P. droned on. He was telling the story of the tracking device removed from an embassy car and attached to the collar of a stray dog, as if it had happened to him. He kept talking until Ian moved one of the little robotic bugs on the workbench to make room for his elbows.

W.P. said, "Hands off! That's part of a special project. Don't mess with my stuff!"

W.P. looked like a mother confronting a child molester. He pushed the little robotic bug out of reach and glared at Ian. "Enough already. I can't spend all afternoon with you. I have more important things to do."

W.P. looked at his watch as Ian got up to leave, then had second thoughts about letting the new boy off early. Why give him a break?

"Hold on. You might as well spend the rest of the day learning something useful."

W.P. put the robotic bug to bed in a fitted foam-lined container, then thought of a way to put the new boy in his place.

"I want you to do a visual search for bugs in one of the empty offices. Muriel is at the trade show, so do hers. A visual search won't find sophisticated eavesdropping devices, but make notes of what you cover and we'll go over them together later. You might learn something. If you're lucky you may get a taste of Muriel's Magic Mouthwash. Think of it as a learning experience."

The visual search was a joke, of course, the equivalent of sending a young soldier out for one hundred yards of skirmish line, or the new girl on the engineering staff down to the machine shop for a ten-inch wang. W.P. had served with Muriel on another posting and was having some fun at the new boy's expense.

Muriel was Muriel Blair, a senior staff member in the front office, the official side of the consulate where the movers and shakers had status. She was forty-two, looked thirty-five, and enjoyed what she called her "little adventures." She wasn't promiscuous, but felt that she had as much right to a varied and multifaceted love life as any man. She was aggressive, and used to having her way in the sexual arena.

She had just been promoted and reassigned from a post in Italy where the Italian men had fallen all over themselves for tall, blonde Muriel. She was now ripe for a new adventure, but German men were more restrained than the Italians, at least the acceptable ones she had met so far.

Ian was under her desk removing the faceplates on the telephone outlets looking for duplex couplers when Muriel came back from the trade show. Ian was a male spider under a desk in the web of an alpha female, though he hadn't seen it that way at the time.

At the time, it had been exciting.

Muriel's office was on the second floor, a quiet corner for a senior official who spent most of her time away at meetings and other consulate business not directly connected to the routine activities on the first floor. Her office featured handcrafted furniture, fine fabrics, muted colors and several original bird prints by Phillip Ashley. All befitting her status, as was the gray silk suit she was wearing when she returned early from the trade show, though Ian could only see the lower half of it from his position beneath her desk.

Muriel walked over and nudged his foot with the toe of her shoe.

"What's going on under there? Are you planting a bug, or taking one out? I hope it's not one of W.P.'s nasty little critters."

All Ian could see of Muriel now was a pair of high heels and sheer stockings. He couldn't get out from under the desk until she moved, and if there was an accepted procedure for talking to the knees of a woman who outranked him, he didn't know the protocol.

Muriel pulled her chair away from the desk, sat down, kicked off her shoes and leaned over.

"Hey, Ian, are you asleep? It looks cozy down there, but we don't know each other well enough to hold meetings under a desk. At least not yet. Get up here."

That one-sided conversation set the stage for their relationship. Muriel was in charge from the beginning, though it wasn't all one way. They were proper in public, erotic in private, and soon engaged in sexual adventures that Muriel referred to as "meetings."

Their meetings took place in Muriel's office at first. Quick encounters on the mauve leather sofa, on the counter in her private bathroom, even once on her desk as a symbolic rite of passage as the affair developed. Most of their meetings began with a nip of Muriel's Magic Mouthwash, mint-flavored vodka stored in an empty mouthwash bottle in her private bathroom. The meetings sometimes ended with Magic Mouthwash too, depending on what they'd been doing.

They knew they couldn't get away with that for long. Sooner or later someone would walk in on them at the office, or perhaps one of W.P.'s little robotic bugs would crawl up the wall outside and look in the window, or peek under the bathroom door.

They were having a nip of Magic Mouthwash in the bathroom after a countertop conference when Muriel came up with the answer. As usual, she was in charge.

"I've arranged for a place to meet. I've been buying the Ashley bird prints from a lady who has a gallery in the old part of town. The gallery is on the way to just about everywhere I go, and who the hell knows where you go when you leave the office? We can meet there in the afternoon, with no one the wiser. I'll give you the address and telephone number."

"I don't know anything about birds, or bird art."

"I'll teach you everything you need to know. Be there at three o'clock. I've made all the arrangements, so be on time."

Ian arrived early to scope out the territory, the habit already established. The gallery wasn't really a gallery, it was more like a small salon. The old lady who owned it led him to a small private viewing room off the main hallway, unlocked the door, stood aside as he entered, then winked at him and said she'd be back when his lady friend arrived.

The room was furnished with a lighted easel for displaying original prints, an ornate love seat for relaxed viewing, and a matching end table with several drawers. Ian walked around the room looking for one-way mirrors and obvious bugs, the best he could do under the circumstances. He checked what looked like a corner closet. It was actually a small bathroom with old-fashioned ornate fixtures. He didn't see anything suspicious, but a visual inspection alone was no guarantee that the room wasn't bugged.

He looked under the love seat, then sat down and went through the drawers of the end table. Like a professional burglar searching a bedroom dresser, he began with the bottom drawer and worked his way up. He found wine glasses nestled in linen napkins, a corkscrew, several boxes of tissues, a bottle of spot remover and a small tin box of powerful pink mints. The gallery owner was a good hostess, if nothing else.

When Muriel arrived, the owner brought in a folder of prints to display on the lighted easel, then turned off the other lights in the room. She told them to bolt the door, so they wouldn't be disturbed. Muriel thanked the old woman, kissed her on the cheek, and bolted the door behind her.

Ian said, "Are you sure this is safe? How well do you know this woman?"

"It's safer than at the office. I met her through my predecessor, and she never had any problems. The old dear has a soft spot for lovers."

"So this is a traditional trysting place. How nice. That makes me feel a lot better."

Muriel said, "Hey, don't get huffy. We all know you guys pass off your local squeezes to the guys who replace you. All I did was pick up the option on a place to meet."

"How does this work?"

"We're expected to buy a print as payment for using the room. The prints are well worth the price, so the use of the room is a bonus."

They used the room off and on for several months. He usually arrived early, and Muriel was often late, so he had time to talk with the old woman, a gentle soul. She loved "the nature," especially birds, and her passion gradually rubbed off on him. He started his own collection of bird prints, added some photographs to the folder, and began taking pictures of birds on his own during his free time. He discovered that much of the surveillance equipment he used in his work as a counterintelligence officer, and many of the covert techniques he employed on the job, worked just as well for wildlife photography. As his birding skills developed, the line between the two became blurred.

His meetings with Muriel might have continued for the rest of his tour of duty if it hadn't been for the dancing lessons, or rather the lack of them. He couldn't dance, at least not to Muriel's standards, and she was used to having her way. She began by kidding him about it, then quit kidding.

"Hey, fella, get with the program. I like to dance, and all I'm asking is that you take a few lessons so you'll be an acceptable partner when I need one at public functions."

"You're a good-looking woman; I'm sure there are plenty of men who would like to dance with you."

"You miss the point. It's not what they want, it's what I want. I want you available so I don't look like someone hard up for a partner."

"You know I don't like to dance, but I'll make an appearance if you think it's that important."

"You still don't get it. I don't want you to show up and march around the dance floor like a good soldier doing his duty. I want you to look like someone who likes to dance, and is good at it."

"But I don't like to dance, and I've never been good at it. I always feel awkward."

"You can learn. We look good together, and you'll do fine on the dance floor, once you get past the awkward stage."

Muriel kept after him. He kept saying no to dancing lessons, and she kept insisting. It wasn't really that important to him one way or another, but he felt the need to assert himself, if only on a minor matter.

It came to a head at an afternoon meeting at the gallery. Muriel made love as if punishing him for not letting her have her way, something she'd never done before. He knew it was a turning point in their relationship, and told her so. He suggested they take a break, and let things cool down for a while.

Muriel had been drinking Magic Mouthwash all afternoon, so it took a minute for his words to sink in. She knew it wasn't the dancing lessons. Lover's quarrels were often about trivial things, at least on the surface. It went deeper than that, and she didn't need him to explain it. Who did he think he was? She'd never been able to take rejection gracefully, and she wasn't about to start now.

"You bastard! Are you trying to dump me? Who do you think you are? I'll decide when this relationship is over, not you!"

She hit him with the mouthwash bottle, spilling the rest of the contents down the front of his trousers, then followed him out to the street as he made an embarrassing mint-soaked getaway. That was just for starters, there was worse to come.

He took a taxi back to the consulate and climbed out of the cab still reeking of Magic Mouthwash just as Muriel drove into the courtyard. He didn't see her in time to get out of the way as she tried to run him down. The front wheel of her Mercedes ran over his left foot as he scrambled for safety.

Muriel stuck her head out the window of her car and yelled, "Ian, you bastard, let's see how fast on your feet you are now. Dance, you creep!"

She took another run at him, but he limped to the middle of the courtyard and she couldn't turn the car sharply enough to do more damage. She went round and round, cursing and calling him names. He could only stand there, reeking of mint vodka.

Muriel finally gave up and drove away, but he'd never lived it down. They'd smoothed it over, he hadn't pressed charges, but the story took on a life of its own as years went by. It became as much a part of legation legend as W.P.'s bugging stories, only no one else claimed that this one had happened to them.

Muriel and he had gone their separate ways, hers onward and upward, his horizontal. She had left the foreign service and was now back in the U.S. and active in politics at the national level. He saw her on television from time to time, and in the local papers. She was in town with some people from her political party, and was aging far better than he was. He made no effort to contact her.

He never developed the skills of a politico, the most basic of which is knowing when to keep your mouth shut, especially in meetings. When the politicos dithered he said things like, "Actions are what count. The rest is just linguistic illusion." At another important meeting he spoke out against decisions based entirely on the reports of "anal-ists," people at the end of the informational digestive track, then found out the politico who had called the meeting was a former analyst.

Ian was a skeptic in a cynical world. It was easier and safer to be a cynic.

Cynics didn't have to prove anything; they'd already made up their minds. Cynics *knew* you couldn't trust anyone, everyone was on the take, and all spouses cheated on their partners. Skeptics searched for *proof*. That was hard work, and often dangerous for the searcher.

Ian made his masters nervous. Most of the promotions went to politicos, or their apprentices. He was successful as a counterintelligence officer, but usually as a number two to someone who had him do most of the work, and then took most of the credit. This number two status froze his career in place. He was good in the field, but considered a pain in the ass at the office.

All that remained of those days was his interest in birds, his collection of bird prints, and a limp that got worse as he got older. He'd been offered early retirement and some part-time work as a field consultant, the best he could do under the circumstances. His handling official gave the impression that he was lucky to get even part-time work.

So here he was, years later, sitting in the evening sun on a park bench at the zoo, massaging his ankle, waiting for the students to arrive for his class on "Wildlife Surveillance With Camera & Recorder."

Spy School.

Chapter 3
Spy School

Ian was still sitting on the bench by the zoo entrance when Maggie arrived.

"Can I talk to you for a minute? Adrian's gone missing again."

Maggie Warren was usually among the first to arrive for the evening class. She and her grandson, Adrian, sometimes arrived together, though Adrian didn't show up for class very often.

Maggie was a wiry little woman with a face that showed the effects of an active outdoor life. She wore well-washed Army fatigues and a faded bush hat with the grace of an old soldier. Now retired from the service, she did shorebird research as a volunteer out on the coast. She had lost a son to drugs, and now had only Adrian, her grandson. Adrian's mother had married again, moved to Europe, and begun a new life that didn't include the boy.

Maggie led Ian out to her Jeep in the parking lot. The Jeep

was easy to identify; it had bumper stickers proclaiming the environmentalist's creed, The Round World Rules. The sticker read, "Everything Has To Go Somewhere - Everything Touches Everything Else." The Jeep also had special off-road tires, and a license plate holder that read, "mud buggy."

Maggie said, "Adrian's missing again."

"He's done this before?"

"Yes, but this time it's different. He came to my place for dinner night before last, left about ten o'clock, and was supposed to call me the next morning. He was acting mysterious, but promised to tell me about it later. He always keeps in touch with me, even when he forgets to call his mother."

"Have you called the police?"

"I did that the first time he dropped out of sight. He turned up a week later on a bus trip to Mexico with a girl he met on the Internet through a local birding group. I apologized to the police for wasting their time, but I don't think they had actually done anything to find him."

"You've called around?"

"Yes, everyone I can think of. I also stopped by his place, but he wasn't there. His roommate says he moved out two weeks ago, but he doesn't know where. I can't believe Adrian would move and not tell me about it, unless he was in some kind of trouble."

"Do you have any idea where he might go, or what he was up to?"

"No, but he left a gym bag in the back. Take a look. You'll see why I'm worried."

Maggie opened the back of the Jeep to reveal the camera and sound equipment she brought to class, and some of the gear she used in her volunteer work on the shorebird project. There was also an Army entrenching tool, a small folding shovel people keep in their vehicles to dig themselves out when they get stuck in the mud. She took good care of her equipment; even the entrenching tool was oiled and sharpened. Army training stayed with you for life, if they got you young enough.

Maggie opened Adrian's gym bag. It contained a pair of spy-shop binoculars with a built-in digital camera, a directional microphone with headphones, a collapsible tripod and some compact disks with anti-government titles.

Maggie said, "This spy-store equipment is crap, but it could get him in trouble. I think he's been playing James Bond."

"This stuff could also be used for birding. Are you sure he wasn't going to bring these items to class?"

"He wasn't coming back to class. He was off on some secret project, and I can't just sit around doing nothing when he may be in trouble. I need your help."

"I'm not a policeman."

Maggie said, "I know what you are. I also know the difference between a pretext, a cover story and a legend. You're running some sort of field operation, with birding as cover. I don't care what, I left all that behind when I retired, but it means you still have contacts. You have access to local and national databases, and a lot of other things. Adrian's into something he won't talk about, even with me, and that scares me."

"He probably just wants to surprise you with his new project, whatever it is, but I can make some phone calls. You should keep calling too. A friend who didn't know anything yesterday may know something now."

"Then you'll help?"

"I'll do what I can. People will be showing up for my class pretty soon, so we can start there. Make your follow-up calls, then come to class. Let's see what turns up."

"Any other suggestions?"

"You mentioned a girl he met through an Internet newsgroup. You could check with the group later."

Maggie got in the Jeep to make her follow-up calls. Ian walked back inside the zoo to use his cell phone, and to watch for the arrival of the other members of the class. He walked to a quiet spot where he could see the new exhibit under construction at the aviary, and still see the zoo entrance.

Laura Cole was in charge of the new exhibit at the aviary, and already at work inside the enclosure. She seemed like a pleasant person, and had an earthy outdoor look he liked, but his interest was apparently not reciprocated.

He'd seen Laura talking with Adrian before class on two occasions when Adrian came early with Maggie, got bored, and wandered around the zoo talking to people. Laura was also friends with two of the younger women who were taking his class, but was barely civil to him. She wasn't easy to talk to, but he gave it another try.

"How's the project going?"

Laura had her back to him when he spoke, had the beginning of a smile on her face when she turned, then let her face go blank when she saw who it was.

"The project is fine. What you see is what you get. What do you want?"

"I'm looking for Adrian. His grandmother is worried about him. She hasn't heard from him in a couple of days, and I wondered if you had seen him around."

"He's a sweet boy, but I've only talked to him a few times. I haven't seen him lately."

"Can you think of anyone who might know more?"

"No. As I said, I hardly know him."

"Have you seen him with anyone else here at the zoo, someone who isn't in my class? I'll check with the class later."

"No." Laura frowned. "That's the third time I've said 'no'. Why is it that every time we talk I feel as if I'm being interrogated?"

"I don't mean to…"

"I don't like spies, or people who act like spies."

"I'm not a spy."

"Maybe not, but you encourage them. We both know that 'Wildlife Surveillance with Camera & Recorder' is just another name for 'Spy School'. You know damned well that's what attracts most of your students, and allows you to charge the fees you do. Two of my zoo volunteers take your class, though God knows why. They're good people, but I wouldn't trust some of the others. That sleazy private eye in your class should be put away."

"Maggie's worried about Adrian. I'm just trying to help."

"For a fee, I suppose."

"No, not for a fee. Adrian will probably turn up in a day or two, but Maggie is concerned, so I'm trying to help. Wouldn't you do the same?" Laura left her work and came over to Ian's side of the enclosure. "Yes, of course I'll help. I'm sorry. I don't know anything about you except what I hear from my two volunteers, and they don't have a very high opinion of men. I apologize for the snide remark."

"That's okay. I rub a lot of people the wrong way. Can you think of anyone who might help us find Adrian?"

"I don't know if this means anything, but I did see Adrian at a meat market in the Fremont district a week ago. He didn't see me, and I was in a hurry, so I didn't stop to talk. He picked up several small packages wrapped in butcher paper, and seemed to know the butcher. I don't see how that can help, but I thought it was odd at the time. Young guys don't usually do much cooking, especially starting from scratch."

"I don't know what that means either, but it may make sense later. Thanks for passing it along. You have my card, but I don't know how to contact you. If you give me your phone number I could let you know how this all turns out."

"Thanks for the offer, but I'll probably hear all about it from April and May, my volunteers. You can always reach me here at the zoo, during working hours."

Laura turned back to her work on the exhibit.

Ian heard the slight pause between "here at the zoo" and "during working hours," and knew he was being brushed off. His personal life, such as it was, depended on a one-step-further approach he used to meet interesting women in interesting places, women he couldn't meet any other way. This technique wasn't working very well with Laura, but that wasn't his chief concern at the moment.

Ian looked toward the zoo entrance just as April and May came through the gate. April was younger and prettier, May older and wiser, but close friends nevertheless. Those weren't their real names, of course, his students usually heard about his classes from newsgroup postings, and used the names they used on the Internet, or other names of their own choosing. Like some Native Americans, they used different names for different reasons, at different times in their lives. Ian thought of Laura, and April and May, as "birds of passage," people leaving one life behind and moving on to another. Now in transition himself, he was attracted to birds of passage.

Ramsey, the private investigator, came through the zoo gate next. He had been driving a flashy new yellow Hummer, one of several expensive vehicles he drove, and had probably had trouble finding a parking space for the big beast. When Laura had mentioned, "That sleazy private eye in your class," Ian knew she had meant Ramsey. Ramsey hit on every attractive woman he met, with or without encouragement.

Ramsey had been dating April, expensive prepackaged dates, safe enough so far, but he told so many conflicting stories about himself that the women had become suspicious. Ramsey, April and May, a strange love triangle, at least to an outsider. The fact that May was a self-styled white witch made the relationship even stranger. Witches had never been much of a threat to society, but society had always been a threat to witches. They burned them, drowned them, and pressed them to death with rocks piled on their chests.

Chapter 4
Monkey Puzzle Park

Ian held the evening class in a natural amphitheater to the east of the zoo entrance. This little used portion of the park was dominated by an old Monkey Puzzle tree of unknown origin, though trees of the same type and the same size were found in several of the older city neighborhoods. The trees looked like something twisted together from giant green pipe cleaners, each out-flung arm covered with scales and sharp spikes in place of leaves. They were supposedly unclimbable, even by monkeys, which gave them their name.

The trees were said to date back to just after the Second World War, but no one was sure of the who, what or when. Some people said the salesman sold seedlings out of the back of an old truck one summer, then went away, the Johnny Appleseed of Monkey Puzzle trees. Perhaps that was just an urban legend.

The grassy amphitheater was a good place to hold the evening class, but one couldn't reserve the space, so Ian went out to his car and brought in the materials he would use in class and put them on the center bench to establish his claim to the spot. His *staijikeppi* was enough to intimidate interlopers, at least those who didn't know what it was.

Better known among birders in the U.S. as a "finnstick," his *staijikeppi* was just that, a tall walking stick with a fork at one end to hold a camera or binoculars steady at eye level. Lewis and Clark and other Army officers of their era had their *espontoons* for use as walking sticks on rough terrain, as props to steady a rifle, and as a weapon for close encounters. Ian's finnstick served some of the same functions, but lacked the double-edged blade of an *espontoon*, and so was less useful as a weapon.

Ian leaned his finnstick against the bench in the amphitheater and began to unpack a Questar spotting scope as the class gathered. He usually began class with a short session of show-and-tell to act as an icebreaker for new class members, and to stimulate conversation. He included both low-tech and high-tech items for contrast, in this case the finnstick and the Questar.

"I see you brought a Questar scope. Who are we spying on today?" Ramsey liked to sneak up behind people and catch them by surprise. When they jumped and turned around, he cocked and pointed his finger like a pistol.

Ramsey repeated the question, "Who are we spying on today?" The question was directed at Ian, but in a voice loud enough to attract the attention of the other class members as they entered the grassy amphitheater, Maggie among them. Ramsey's questions were often pointed, but seldom productive, so Ian turned to the class without answering.

Ian outlined what Maggie had told him about Adrian's disappearance, but tried not to unduly alarm the class about something that he thought would probably turn out to be a false alarm. The class members were sympathetic, and promised to call Maggie if they had anything to report.

Ramsey asked if Maggie had checked with the police and the hospitals about unidentified accident victims, and said he, too, would help in the search for Adrian. Ian thought this was odd since Ramsey had always seemed self-centered and an unlikely volunteer.

Maggie seemed reassured by the positive reactions of her classmates. She thanked the class, then left to go back to the parking lot and the privacy of her Jeep to make more phone calls. Since Ian had nothing to add at this point, he got on with the class.

"We've covered the basics of 'Wildlife Surveillance with Camera & Recorder' in previous classes. Today I want to talk about practical applications, the how-tos and why-fors of what we've already learned. We'll start with some low-tech and high-tech show-and-tell. The *staijikeppi* and Questar scope are good examples of the two extremes, so we'll begin there."

Ian spoke for several minutes using his outline of the course and his notes on his laptop to keep him on track. He knew that the class was little more than an entertainment for some of the people in front of him in the amphitheater, but felt obligated to those who were serious about wildlife and wildlife conservation. His class was responsive to different adult learning styles, but people like Ramsey, who saw the world as rectilinear, often had little tolerance for other people's learning preferences. Ramsey claimed he wanted "just the facts," but accepted only his own definition of fact and fiction. He was also dogged. Ian had ignored his earlier question, so when Ian passed around the Questar scope, Ramsey took another try at him.

Ramsey pointed the scope toward April, and then at May,

and said, "So, like I said before, who are we spying on today?"

May said, "A female Merlin falcon has been hunting starlings near Greenlake in lower Woodland. You could go spy on her, since you seem to like looking at females."

Ramsey gave May a dirty look when the class laughed. He pointed the scope at her as if sighting along a rifle barrel. Ramsey always seemed to be pointing something at someone. He spoke to Ian without turning his head, "You expect us to believe they named a bird after Merlin the Magician?"

Ian said, "It's the other way around. Merlin the Magician was named after the falcon. The bird is swift and elusive and often seems to disappear in the field. Merlin falcons are found worldwide. They breed in northern latitudes and migrate to Mexico, South America, the Mediterranean, the Middle East and parts of China. They have two-foot wingspans, and appear uniformly dark in the field. Males are brighter than females with slate-blue wings and backs, dark heads and dull facial markings. They have Rufous undersides marked with dark streaks, and slate-gray tails. Females are brown with light brown streaks on the undersides.

"Merlins nest in woodlands near open areas where they can hunt birds, rodents, insects and small lizards. They sometimes catch birds as large as pigeons, including small shorebirds. They use old crow and magpie nests, and lay up to five eggs. The young may stay together after fledging, and migrate south together. Falconers know the merlins well; they were called the Ladies's Hawk, and were used for hunting small prey in the days before gunpowder. Merlins have been seen here in Woodland Park, in Carkeek Park, and along the steep hillsides below the Pike Place Market."

Ramsey said, "I've been to the Pike Place Market, but I've never seen a Merlin."

"Merlins are small falcons the size of a pigeon with pointed, backswept wings. They move fast, swooping along the hillsides. You have to be quick to see them or take their pictures."

May said, "Ramsey is interested in different birds, the ones in short skirts coming down the long flights of stairs from the market to the waterfront."

Ramsey gave her a dirty look. "I meet clients at the market if they don't want to meet at the office. I do my own thing, and mind my own business. You people should do the same if you want to stay out of trouble."

Ramsey was still pointing the Questar scope at May when Ian walked over to reclaim it. The Pike Place Market was a popular first-time meeting place for people who answered personals ads, and for seasoned philanderers who went there to meet secret lovers. Birders photographed the merlins and the other wildlife along the steep hillsides and down on the waterfront. Private investigators photographed the human wildlife that met next to the brass pig, under the market clock. Ian had no illusions about Ramsey and the private eye business, but he wanted to keep the class on track for the sake of the other students. He took the scope back from Ramsey and ended the show-and-tell portion of the class before things heated up between Ramsey and May.

Ian ignored Ramsey's veiled threat and said, "Merlins are fairly common. Merlins, *falco columbarius,* and barn owls, *tyto alba,* are often used as daytime and nighttime examples of birds found on every continent except Antarctica.

"Barn owls live in abandoned buildings, tree cavities, and as we know from the stories we heard as children, they live in church steeples. Their feathers are buff-colored above, white below, with black or brown speckles. They don't hoot. They hiss, click, make strange snoring sounds and scream. They eat mice and other rodents, insects, small birds, and fish in some parts of the world. Barn owls fly mostly at night, and are silent except for a whisper of wings. They may fly up to three miles looking for food. They mate for life, and adjust the number of eggs and the number of broods in a breeding season, based on the food supply. The normal barn owl brood is three to six young."

Ramsey couldn't let these remarks pass without comment. He said, "So, if you know your merlins and barn owls, you've got your pretexts covered for both day and night operations. They provide a cover story that a spy could use anywhere in the world, any time of the day or night. Ian, you've been around. How was the birding when you worked for Uncle Sam? Who were you spying on when you went out at night on an owl prowl?"

Ian said, "Any birder can be a spy, I suppose. Some people even accuse the birds themselves of spying. A South African stork carrying a tracking device was arrested on suspicion of espionage in Burundi. Locals caught the stork and handed it over to the police. The bird was part of a migration study, and was fitted with a tracking device, an aerial, and a small solar cell to charge the battery. Albatross have been tracked with transmitters in special harnesses on the birds's backs. Peregrine backpacks have a flexible antenna sticking out of the back end of the pack—a strange sight—and enough for a dozen conspiracy theories about the government using birds as spies. Conspiracy buffs say no one has any privacy these days, not even the birds. These stories are interesting, but I don't want to stray too far from our lesson plan. Let's talk about practical applications, the how-tos and why-fors of what we've already learned."

Ian demonstrated some tricks of the trade used by

photographers to steady their cameras for quick shots in the field. He showed the class how to use the forked finnstick to best advantage, how to steady a camera by placing the strap across the back and under the arms and bracing the elbows against the chest so that the whole body is used to steady the shot, and how to take pictures from a vehicle using a camera mount clamped to a rolled-down window. He stayed with the lesson plan until everything in the class prospectus for that day had been covered.

When he talked about Internet resources, as he did toward the end of each class, one of the serious birders who always sat at the back raised her hand and asked a question. She had done an Internet search using key words associated with the mating habits of birds, and had learned that some birds eavesdrop on each other. The reference she found had been incomplete, but had mentioned one bird in particular.

She asked Ian what he knew about Great Tits.

It was a serious question, but Ian saw that some class members weren't taking it seriously. He knew that Ramsey, or one of the other disruptive people in the group, would take over the conversation if he didn't act quickly.

Ian looked toward the birder at the back of the class and said, "The female Great Tit (*parus major*) evaluates potential mates by eavesdropping on the territorial singing contests among the males. Male singing ability is apparently directly related to pair success, so eavesdropping is important. Female chickadees do the same thing, according to researchers."

To head off other disruptive reactions along the same lines, he mentioned birding research in Denmark regarding the female barn swallow's preference for males with long tails before someone else brought it up. The length of the male barn swallow's (*hirundo rustica*) tail feathers is an indication of his overall health and desirability as a mate. Ian talked about the research and the scientific process involved, but couldn't avoid the obvious conclusion voiced by one of the troublemakers who said, "What you mean is the females like lots of tail!"

With that out of the way, Ian asked if anyone else had found any Internet sites of interest. May raised her hand. She mentioned a spy-shop website, and asked if the miniscopes used by private investigators were useful for birding. Ian knew this was aimed at Ramsey, but he couldn't stop her from talking.

May said, "The spy-shop websites sell some of the same binoculars and spotting scopes birders use, but they also sell little miniscopes you can hide in the palm of your hand so that sneaky people can spy on other people without being caught. They say all a private eye has to do is put his hand up to his face to look through the miniscope without attracting attention. They show a guy leaning on the railing overlooking the beach where the girls are sunbathing. Miniscopes can't be much good for birding, but I saw Ramsey with one the other day, so I could be wrong about that. What about it, Ramsey?"

Ramsey was furious at May's remarks. "I don't know what the hell you're talking about, and neither do you! Keep your nose out of other people's business, and your mouth shut! This is your last warning!"

"Is that a threat?"

"Take it any way you want to. You're the one causing the problem! You use words like weapons, then act surprised when a guy protects himself. I don't have to put up with this crap."

May started to say something in reply, but Ramsey turned on Ian and drowned her out. "Can't you control this broad? I don't pay good money to be harassed by some bitch who admits she's a witch. I've had enough of this shit. You know what you can do with your stupid class!"

Ramsey stalked out of the amphitheater as Ian tried to smooth things over. It did no good, for May left soon after. She left without April, which was odd as they usually came and went in May's car.

Ian said, "That's enough for today," and dismissed the class, but a few people lingered to talk as they always did. Ian gathered his gear and hurried toward the parking area in hopes of intervening if Ramsey and May confronted each other on their way to their cars.

Ramsey's big yellow Hummer and May's little SUV were both gone from the parking lot by the time he got there.

Chapter 5
The Secret of Secrets

Ian locked his gear in the trunk of his car and met Maggie near the zoo entrance.

Maggie said, "What was that all about? I was still on the phone in the Jeep when Ramsey drove past me like a madman. I thought he was going to run me over."

Ian said, "Ramsey and May got into a fight in class. He threatened her, and then stomped out. May left right after. I went to see that they didn't continue the fight in the parking lot, but they'd left by the time I got there. How long since he drove off?"

"Just a few minutes."

"Did you see May?"

"No, but she could have parked at the other end of the lot, and gone out the other entrance. All I saw was Ramsey and the yellow Hummer."

Ian said, "What about your calls? Did you find Adrian?"

"No, no one's seen him. Everyone's nice about it, but they all seem to think he's just goofing off, like the last time he disappeared. I don't think so, and I'm going to keep on looking."

Laura was still at work on the new outdoor exhibit under construction at the aviary. She waved to them from inside the enclosure, then went around inside the building and came out the side door. She ignored Ian, but hugged Maggie and asked about Adrian. Maggie told her what she knew, and received a promise of help in return. April joined in the conversation.

The three women made an interesting group, Maggie the old soldier, Laura the zoo architect, and April the party girl. Though very different, they had at least one thing in common, as Ian soon saw. They didn't need him, or anyone else, to help them make decisions. Maggie had her own ideas about what to do to find Adrian, and was willing to force the issue. She knew that the police most often help those who help themselves and was already putting together a flyer with Adrian's picture and contact information. She was on her way to a copy shop, and offered April a ride since she was going in the direction of April's apartment. They said goodby to Laura and left with a wave and a smile for him, almost as an afterthought. Ian expected the same from Laura and was surprised when she invited him into the aviary.

As they walked toward the side door, Laura said, "Maggie told me she thinks Adrian is playing spy. Did he learn that from you?"

"No. I never talked about spying with him."

"But you didn't discourage him either. Everyone knows that the wildlife surveillance techniques you teach in class can also be used in espionage. Playing spy is part of the attraction for your students."

Ian said, "I suppose it depends on your point of view, how you describe what you do for a living, and how you live your life.

We're all spies, in a manner of speaking. Research, investigative reporting, hunting for the truth, whatever you want to call it, it's at the center of intellectual life, and often involves some form of subterfuge. We all have our hidden agendas, our personal secret of secrets."

"You say subterfuge, but you mean lying. When I told a fib as a child my mother would always remind me of the poem about the tangled web we weave when we practice to deceive."

"My father was an intelligence officer. He would have agreed with your mother, but would have added that 'all our friends would soon be dead, if our foes were not misled'."

Laura unlocked the side door of the aviary, and led the way. Ian knew this wasn't a social call, and wondered why he was there. She went to a vending machine in the hallway and bought them both coffee. The building was shutting down for the day, but the snack bar was still open, so it seemed odd that Laura didn't go there. He swirled his coffee around in the paper cup to mix in the artificial creamer, and looked for security cameras. He always did that; it was automatic. Another quote from his childhood popped into his head, something about habit being a cable that we weave a thread of each day, until it becomes too strong to break.

The only security camera in the hallway was aimed at the snack bar entrance, which meant the vending machine was out of camera range. Laura apparently didn't want to be on camera, at least not yet.

She leaned on the wall next to the vending machine, and sipped her coffee. She was still wearing work clothes—denim shirt, jeans, and boots—but seemed in no hurry to change, or to go to her office. Ian waited her out. People eventually got to the point, but often talked about something else first while they worked up their courage.

Laura swirled her coffee as he had done, then peered into the cup as if looking for answers there. Ian stood still, and kept quiet. After a minute or so of silence, she said, "So tell me, why do people spy? Does anyone know for sure?"

Ian wondered if she was leading up to something, or just making idle conversation while she waited for the building to shut down for the day. Patience was one of his few virtues, an easy one to exercise under the circumstances. Laura had barely been civil to him before, but now she had come to him on her own. He was more than willing to make conversation, even if nothing came of it.

He said, "Most spies, at least the ones we know about, are motivated by money, idealism, alienation and adventure, not necessarily in that order. Government spies get the most attention, but there are probably more spies in the private sector. Political terrorists, religious fanatics and common criminals of every kind have their own agendas, although they often use some of the same methods of operation."

"Like what?"

"Pretext attacks, for example. All spies need inside information, and using a pretext is often the easiest way to get it."

"April said you talked about pretexts in class today—birding pretexts."

"One of the people in class mentioned pretexts. I didn't bring up the subject, and it isn't part of the course. I certainly didn't encourage Adrian to spy, if that's what he's doing. I'm not as bad as you think I am."

"Not as bad as I think you are? That's what Maggie said while you were gone, though it sounds like faint praise, at best."

Ian remembered part of a famous quotation, something about being "damned by faint praise," but he couldn't remember who said it. Damned or not, he was glad when Laura smiled and changed the subject.

"What do you do when you're not teaching birding classes? That can't be a full-time job."

"I'm a security consultant. I help companies protect their business secrets and other intellectual assets. It's a management function usually referred to as business espionage controls and countermeasures."

"That sounds more exciting than teaching birding classes."

"It's mostly lies and lawyers. That's true before, during and after the event, including those rare occasions when a spy is actually brought to trial."

He spoke in general terms about his work as Laura looked up and down the hall and the building gradually emptied. She now seemed more interested in espionage than birding. It was obvious she had been asking Maggie and April about what he covered in class, and what they knew about his other work. As the building grew quiet she poured the last of her coffee down the drain in the vending machine, crumbled the paper cup, and threw it in the trash. He did the same. The gesture signaled a turning point in the conversation.

Laura said, "Will you take a walk with me? I've got something to show you. It may be nothing, but it's weird and I don't know who else to ask. Maggie says I can trust you."

He said, "What's the problem?"

"I may be paranoid, but I think Ramsey has been spying on me. I think he planted a bug outside the enclosure where I've been working."

"Have you told zoo security?"

"No. I'm not on staff here, I came in from outside as part of the remodeling team. I don't want to be labeled as some kind of nut, especially this early in the project. I need to talk to someone though, and you're the logical person."

"You're sure he planted a bug?"

"I saw him do it."

"Have you inspected the device?"

"No, another man removed it a short time later, at least I think he did. I saw Ramsey plant it, but I couldn't find it when I went out there after the other guy left. Why plant a bug and then have someone else remove it? It must still be there. It makes no sense to me, but I can show you the spot and you can see for yourself."

"Before you do that you had better tell me exactly what happened. Start at the beginning."

The aviary was built around a central gallery that was open to the public during the day. The glass-fronted exhibits faced inward and featured natural settings. Most of the exhibits were completely enclosed and climate-controlled to accommodate tropical birds, but the exhibit Laura was working on was for native birds that were used to the local weather conditions. This exhibit extended from the inside viewing area through to an outside enclosure to give the native birds more room, and the viewers more options.

Laura led him along the gallery to a point where they could look through from the inside exhibit to the outside enclosure. The visitors were gone for the day and gallery lights had already been dimmed.

Laura said, "Ramsey comes and goes at the zoo as he pleases, because of the city bird project. He watches the women—nothing illegal as far as I know—but enough to make all of us nervous. Most of us stay as far away from him as we can. I was coming back through the gallery after a break when I happened to look through here and saw Ramsey plant something near the outside enclosure. It only took a second."

"Could you see what it was?"

"No, but I think he put it where the handrail connects to the stone wall along the outside of the enclosure. As I say, it only took a second."

"Then what happened?"

"That's even weirder. After he planted the thing Ramsey came around inside to where we are now, looking through to the outside enclosure. A little while later this other man went to the same spot outside, leaned on the wall, and then went away. I have no idea what he was doing."

"What did the outside man look like?"

"An Asian, I think, but he was wearing a sweatshirt with the hood up, so I could only see part of his face."

"What did Ramsey do?"

"He watched the guy outside come and go, and then left himself a few minutes later. He wasn't in any hurry."

"What did you do?"

"I waited awhile, and then went to the spot outside, but I didn't find anything. I'm not really sure what I saw, or what to do about it. I do know Ramsey is some kind of a private eye, and I don't trust the bastard."

"Have you seen anything suspicious since then?"

"No, but the more I thought about what happened, the stranger it seemed. Maggie said I should talk to you, and show you where the bug was planted."

"I'll take a look, but I don't want you with me. Wait here. If the zoo security people come around and ask questions, tell them I'm here to inspect your work. I'll carry the clipboard I use for my notes in class, and try to look official."

"Shouldn't we go to my office first? I could call security from there and tell them what you're doing."

"You're better off here in the public gallery, at least for now.

You're within range of the security cameras, and I won't be far away. Give me your keys so I can come and go without setting off the security alarms."

"You're starting to scare me."

"You're okay here. This may not take long."

Ian took Laura's keys and went out the side entrance. He inspected the fencing, handrail and wall connectors, made notes on the clipboard, frowned, shook his head and looked officious. He then took a closer look at the metal fasteners that held the enclosure together, the handrail supports along the outside of the exhibit, and the brackets that connected the handrail to the stone wall at the side of the enclosure. The natural light was beginning to fade so he used a small flashlight and fiber optic probe from his bag for this part of the inspection. The whole thing took less than twenty minutes.

He didn't find an eavesdropping device, and hadn't expected to find one. There was a small crack in the rock underneath the handrail where it connected to the stone wall, but it hadn't been used as a place to hide a bug, he felt sure of that. Eavesdropping success depended on planting an audio/ video device in a good location, and this wasn't a good location. Outside weather conditions, the high probability that a device would be discovered if left in place for long, and the distance from potential targets all made this an unlikely place to plant a bug. As is the rule for so many human endeavors, the first three things an eavesdropper must consider are location, location and location.

Laura wasn't being bugged, at least not at this part of her work site. What she saw, or at least thought she saw, was probably a "drop," though he couldn't prove it. Ramsey had dropped off a small object, a floppy computer disk or a memory card from a digital camera, in the crack in the wall. The other man had picked it up a short time later. The zoo was a good place to make a quick drop and move on, a public place open to everyone, including foreign tourists.

Ramsey had been watching from inside the building to see that the drop was picked up, a dangerous move, something an experienced agent wouldn't do under normal circumstances. Agents don't usually hang around drop sites because they know that sudden and unexpected movement is the best cover, and the best way to stay a step ahead of the opposition. Ramsey had made a drop, and then stayed around to observe the pickup. He must have had a good reason.

Was Ramsey and the other man involved in espionage? What Laura saw wasn't proof of illegal activity, but then why would a private eye act like a spy? He didn't know, but he had to tell Laura something. He went back inside the gallery.

Ian said, "There's nothing there now, no eavesdropping device, and nothing else suspicious. You're not being bugged, at least not at that location. I don't think you have anything to worry about."

"Do you believe me when I say I saw Ramsey plant something out there?"

"Yes, I believe you."

"Then why shouldn't I worry? What is it that you're not telling me?"

"What you saw was probably a drop and a pickup. Ramsey dropped off something and the other man picked it up. Something small, perhaps a small amount of drugs for personal use. I doubt it had anything to do with you, that's just a good spot for a drop."

Laura said, "You're sure?"

"As sure as I can be, based on what you saw."

"And you're an expert on this spooks-and-spies stuff?"

"I'm always leery of people who call themselves experts."

"That's not much of an answer, and not very reassuring."

"If you like, I can give you the name of a reliable electronic countermeasures technician to check your office for bugs. There are a few good ones in the private sector, though most deal in smoke and mirrors."

"Maggie says I can trust you, so I guess I should also trust your judgment."

"We don't have to leave it at that. I'm sure you saw something. Call me if you see anything else suspicious, day or night. You have my phone number."

"Only your business number."

"All of my calls are routed through that number, then forwarded on to me."

"That's what spies do, isn't it? Everyone kept at arms length, everything at one remove."

"This isn't business, at least not as far as I'm concerned. We've both had a busy day, we're both tired, so let's not end this conversation by taking potshots at each other. You can call me anytime. Call if you're worried. Call if you just want to talk. You have my card."

Ian could see that the conversation had taken a turn for the worse, and could only go downhill from there. He wanted to leave on a positive note, so he smiled and made eye contact with Laura as he shook her hand. He left without looking back.

Why would a private eye act like a government spy? The question sounded poetic, at least it did after Ian had a glass of wine at the kitchen counter of the house he was house-sitting for a friend away on assignment. The house wasn't much an investment at best, but less impersonal than a motel, and a place to have something to eat in private and do his paperwork. Ian grilled a cheese sandwich in chive oil and ate it over the kitchen sink so as not to drip oil on the kitchen floor. He often ate over the kitchen sink in other people's houses. A can of sardines in mustard sauce while looking out into someone's back garden, a deli salad eaten while looking over the rooftops from the kitchen of someone else's apartment. There was something comforting about kitchens, even when they didn't belong to you.

After eating, he took a bird book out of his airline bag, checked his e-mail, and changed his e-mail password. He changed passwords often. Any book's index can be used as a random password generator by picking a page of your choice and using the odd mix of letters and numbers that run down the page at the uneven ends of each index's listing. He used bird books as password generators because there were several to choose from, and they fit his lifestyle.

Why would a private eye act like a government spy? he wondered, and so would others with more resources than he had, and a better chance of success. He poured a second glass of wine and called his handling official.

Part-time work was better than none, even under these conditions.

Chapter 6
Bird of Passage

May was a bird of passage, a person leaving one life behind and moving on to another. Like some Native Americans, she had used different names for different reasons, at different times in her life. May was the name of the moment. She thought of herself as a migratory bird, an Arctic Plover pehaps, flying from pole to pole as the rhythms of life dictated. The victim of a bad romantic relationship, she was moving on toward what she hoped was a new and better life.

She called herself a white witch, but was drawn to the magical world it represented, rather than ritual witchcraft. Her involvement with witchcraft was little more than wearing silver bracelets and using special lotions to scent-mark the people she touched so that she would be remembered.

May was also an amateur surveillant, a skill she put to good use whenever her friend April found a new man in class, or through the personals ads. April would meet the man in a public place for coffee, then go home by herself. May would follow the man after the meeting to see if he was who he said he was. If he went home, she would take pictures of his house or apartment building, and scout the neighborhood. She always learned something, even if the man just drove to a bar. A man's vehicle, and what one could see inside it when it was parked, often revealed a lot.

May called what she did, "Checking Up on Mr. Wonderful," though she hadn't had much luck checking up on Ramsey. She joked about it, but was motivated by a real concern for her friend, April. She knew that some of the men April met weren't who they said they were, and that April needed her protection. April was a small town girl, and a bit naïve, at least by May's standards.

April had been attracted by Ramsey's forceful self assurance, an attribute shared by gangsters and other dangerous men that some women find appealing, at least at first. April's first real date with Ramsey was a dinner cruise on a chartered yacht, a safe setting for what should have been a pleasant evening, but which turned into a sparring match. April asked questions, and Ramsey talked a lot, but always in circles. He bragged of his success inventing and selling sophisticated electronics equipment to government agencies, which, of course, he wasn't allowed to name. He was actually a used equipment salesman, among other things. He bought used TSCM equipment from private investigators and others who were going out of business, then sold it to a never-ending crop of new investigators and other technical surveillance countermeasures wannabes. The markups were fantastic. Ramsey was well-off financially, but seldom used checks or company credit cards that could be traced, and paid for most things in cash.

May had been suspicious from the start. She had tried following him twice, but couldn't keep up with the BMW he had been driving at the time.

This evening was different. When Ramsey pulled out of the zoo's parking lot after class he was driving his big yellow Hummer, and she had her SUV. The SUV hadn't been fast enough to keep up with his BMW, but she thought it was fast enough for the Hummer.

She gave Ramsey a half-block start as he left the zoo's parking lot because the person you were following was most likely to spot you when they first checked their mirrors as they pulled into traffic. She let him merge with the stream of traffic, then moved up a little closer and settled in for the chase. The daylight was going fast, but she was used to nighttime driving. The "Mr. Wonderfuls" usually came out after dark. Ramsey hadn't expected a tail, but after he cooled down from his confrontation with May at Spy School, he began his usual counter-surveillance maneuvers. He checked his rearview mirrors without turning his head, moved to the right side of the street and slowed down as if about to make a turn, and watched to see if anyone behind him reacted.

Basic stuff, part of a counter-surveillance checklist he kept in his head.

His first indication that he was being followed was when he pulled into an empty driveway on a quiet street to turn around and saw headlights behind him at the intersection. He got out of the Hummer, walked around to the back of the empty house, and came up around the other side of the building just in time to see May cruise by. She didn't see him, but he knew she saw the Hummer. She drove halfway down the block, pulled over in front of a van that hid her car from view, and turned off her lights.

Ramsey couldn't believe it. The bitch had him under surveillance! He would now have to deal with her one way or another, and that meant trouble. He shouldn't have let Irving Cordell talk him into attending the Spy School in the first place. It made no sense since he already knew more about that shit than the instructor, including the latest info on digiscoping. Lawyers like Cordell were always so damn devious, even with their own people. He hadn't learned anything new at Spy School, and hadn't expected to, but Irving still insisted on daily reports.

The class was full of mud people and other assholes; there was probably even a Jew or two. They were all troublemakers. First Adrian, the kid on the ledge, a papist. Now May, a witch, one of the ungodly. They deserved what they got!

Ramsey walked back around the empty house the way he had come, got in the Hummer, and drove away. Sure enough, May followed. He drove to the shopping center north of the zoo, and there she was, three cars back. The Hummer was a girl-getter that fit his image, but it wasn't the ideal counter-surveillance vehicle. It was time to switch cars.

Ramsey drove into the parking lot of the shopping center and left the Hummer under the lights close to the west entrance. He set the kill switch and burglar alarm, and locked the doors. He wasn't about to let some asshole steal his ride while he was busy dealing with the witch. He watched May park five cars back where she had a good view of the Hummer.

He hurried through the shopping center, went out the east entrance, and crossed the street in the middle of the block. *Sudden and unexpected movement was basic to counter-surveillance.* He went down one alley, crossed to another, and from there to a rented garage. He always had at least two rented garages, one for a work car, and another for his RV.

Thank God for old broads with dead husbands! He checked the bulletin boards at the senior centers until he found some old woman who needed to rent her garage so she could keep up the house payments. He paid the garage rent in advance, in cash, put in his own locks and alarms, and had the place to himself. The old broads liked him, never asked any questions, and went to bed early.

He unlocked the garage, went inside, and turned on the nightlight. The garage contained two steel storage lockers—one business, one personal—and the last of a series of older full-size sedans he bought for cash from private parties without transferring the title. When he was done with one of these work cars he wiped it down, parked it in a tough neighborhood, left the keys in it, and walked away. The car soon disappeared, and nobody was the wiser.

Ramsey went first to the business locker to sanitize himself. He had to take care of the witch, but not jeopardize one of his major moneymakers, the lucrative info business with the lawyer, Irving Cordell. He put the audio/video tapes he had taken at Spy School in with the tapes from the financial center, to be delivered later. He had delivered tapes from several of the downtown office buildings. The tapes he took in class with his pager cam were horseshit, lots of crap and a few predigested grains of truth as far as he was concerned. He preferred more direct methods.

Ramsey knew that Cordell must have some important contacts because the money was good, but his own field work was the most important part of the info biz. Irving had him out looking for something that would give him power over the people he targeted in important industries, financial, research, high-tech—the lot—but Irving wasn't the one who found the weaknesses that could be exploited. Ramsey knew he took most of the risks while doing the field work, but you could bet your ass that the lawyer took most of the profits. That would change once he got his hands on the client list. When that happened, it was goodbye, Cordell.

The business locker contained an assortment of tiny board cameras that could be hidden in pagers, pocket radios, baseball caps, or in any of a number of other places. There was also a mini-camcorder that could be secured with a belly-band under his clothes, or placed in a fanny-pack. His toolkit and an assortment of wireless transmitters and other eavesdropping devices took up the rest of the upper shelf space. Climbing gear filled the bottom of the locker. Most of his equipment had legal applications and was available from security equipment suppliers. It was how you used it that made it illegal, but what the fuck, there wasn't much chance of being caught. Besides, nobody got ahead in the world by being strictly legal.

Ramsey moved to his personal locker. The business tapes went to Cordell, but he had extra copies of the "chick pics" for his own collection. He refocused and enhanced the sexual features of the women he photographed, and played the tapes over and over for his own enjoyment. His chick pics of the women's washrooms at the financial center and other downtown office buildings were his alone.

He kept dupes of the audio/video tapes he made for Irving Cordell because who knew when a lawyer might turn against you? He would have the tapes to protect himself if the shit hit the fan and Irving decided to push him in front of it to take the blame by himself. A guy had to take precautions.

Irving paid well and never quibbled about expenses, but he acted so damn superior, like his farts didn't stink. It was his job to catch people off-guard and record their activities with a hidden audio/video bug, but Irving paid the tab, and made it happen.

If the target was a married woman having an affair, he taped her having sex with her lover, made a list of her family, friends and co-workers, and threatened to send copies of the tapes to everyone on the list. He did the same thing if the targeted woman was a closet lesbian, or had some other exploitable weakness. Drinking, drugs, gambling, sex with underage partners, anything the targets didn't want exposed could be used to control them and force them to cough up confidential information. Blackmailing people to obtain business secrets worth millions of dollars made a lot more sense than just cleaning out their bank accounts, especially if the target was a researcher with three kids and a five-year-old car. The same went for the men, of course, but the women were always more fun.

Ramsey looked at his watch and wondered how long May would sit in the shopping center parking lot watching the Hummer. She had to know he'd come back for it sooner or later, but she wasn't a pro and would probably lose interest after an hour or so. He'd better get his ass in gear.

He had several firearms in his personal locker, some legal, some illegal. He tucked a Smith & Wesson airweight he'd bought at a gun show in his belt and started locking up. He liked revolvers because he could get the first shot off one-handed, even while driving, without carrying the weapon cocked and taking a chance of blowing his balls off. He liked guns, but he didn't like holsters, at least not for field work. Why carry a gun in a holster when you might have to ditch it in a hurry, again one-handed, while driving? It took extra seconds to unfasten and ditch a holstered pistol, and seconds were sometimes important, especially if a car with a gumball machine on top was back a few blocks, but coming up fast in your rearview mirror.

Ramsey drove the heavy sedan out into the darkened driveway and finished locking up. An untraceable vehicle and an untraceable weapon were probably a myth in the modern computerized world, but with the sedan and the Smith & Wesson he came as close as he could. The rest was up to the gods of war, and for him, a war it was. He was at war against Muslims, Jews, Papists, Witches and the rest of the ungodly.

He drove back to the shopping center and parked one aisle over from May where he could see her, but she couldn't see him without turning around in her seat. He watched, and he didn't have long to wait. May had been there less than an hour, but had already begun to fidget. She probably had to pee, as women did when they got excited. She watched the Hummer for a few minutes more, then backed out of her parking space and left the lot by the north exit. Ramsey followed in the sedan.

May turned east on the main street, then went off on a cross street that wound past an old railroad overpass and down toward the apartment buildings along the lake. The road predated the city planning commission, was poorly lit, and went its own way along the edge of the embankment.

Ramsey couldn't believe his luck! May was going home after a surveillance, but wasn't even checking her rearview mirror. She'd seen his Hummer back at the shopping center, and it never occurred to her that he might have a second car stashed nearby. That was the difference between a pro and an amateur—the one lived off what never occurred to the other.

He couldn't have set it up better! A winding road at night along the edge of a ravine, a top-heavy little SUV, and a heavy sedan for a ram car. He moved up fast on her left-quarter panel, hit the high beams to blind her, then rammed the SUV from the side just behind the rear wheel. She spun around, went over the edge, rolled twice, and landed upside down at the bottom of the embankment. Even a witch couldn't survive that. There were no witnesses, no suspicious bullet holes for accident investigators to find, and no complications. It couldn't have worked out better!

Ramsey circled south past the old Naval station, came back north, and parked the sedan in the rented garage. He'd now have to dump the sedan; it had a bent bumper and SUV paint on the right front fender, but he'd soon find another work car in the classifieds.

He walked to the shopping center for a drink at a sports bar and watched part of a ball game on the big screen. He knew that May had been no real threat to him or his business, but he didn't regret the killing. It would look like an accident, so he wasn't worried.

He wasn't worried about Adrian, either. He'd pushed the kid off the ledge in the fog, but there had been no reports of a body being found. Maybe the kid had fallen into one of the big industrial dumpsters in the alley and was now buried under tons of garbage in the landfill, a good place for the little shit. No news was good news, so he had apparently gotten away with that too.

He called Irving Cordell to find out where he wanted the videotapes dropped off, and was surprised at the location. He picked up the Hummer and drove downtown.

Psychologists and defense attorneys have their own views of the world, and their own professional agendas. Ramsey's motives for killing May could be debated on many levels, and in many venues, but the fact was that he did what he did because he wanted to. His motivation was as simple as that, as it is with many crimes.

We live in a dangerous world, as every birder knows. Birds face many hazards. If a robin's song sometimes seems sad it's because half his friends have died since last summer. Nature herself may seem cruel, but man is the primary threat to wildlife, and to his fellow humans.

May was a bird of passage. Many birds died on migration.

Chapter 7
Sometimes an Honorable Profession

Attorney Irving Cordell's business was built on a simple premise: *Intelligence gathering is like fishing. Hook a fish and you'll have fish for a day, hook a fisherman and you'll have fish for the life of the fisherman.*

Most secrets are soon outdated, useful only to analysts who try to make sense of them in their reports, and historians who later regurgitate this material in books. Secrets, even perishable ones, are of course important, but the person in whose mind the secret originated is a far better target for espionage. That person will likely build on that secret to produce other secrets, work with other experts in that field, and produce other breakthroughs. Know the person, have a hook in that person, and you can know today's secrets, and where to go for tomorrow's.

Irving had Ramsey planting and servicing eavesdropping devices to obtain derogatory information about people of interest. He was looking for dirty little secrets, but everything derogatory was entered into his private database where it could be checked and cross-referenced to establish both short-term and long-term patterns. A molehill of minor indiscretions could be turned into a mountain of accusations, if a pattern could be developed. Irving would then use this information against that person again and again to force them to do his bidding.

Irving Cordell was a modern-day spy, but referred to himself as a "competitor intelligence professional." He always used competitor intelligence terms to describe himself and his work. He made it clear to prospective clients that eighty to ninety percent of the information they wanted was available from public records and other open sources, then left it up to them to ask for the other ten percent. They usually did.

Ninety percent of something is never enough. Who wants only the first nine chapters of a ten-chapter book? Who would buy a book with the last chapter missing?

One of Irving's best clients was an international banker with a private office in a small building down a quiet side street a few blocks from a park on Capitol Hill. A brass plaque on the black iron gate at the entrance to the courtyard was its only identifying feature. Irving suspected that the banker was a front man for a foreign government, but weren't they all, one way or another? He and the banker were both well-paid for their services, and knew when not to ask questions.

Irving's clients wanted to know their competitors's secrets, and what these competitors were going to do with their secrets. What were their *intentions?* Who were their competitors secretly recruiting, and why? What were they going to do with the funds from their new investors? Where would their new facilities be built? When?

Intentions were the primary target of espionage. That inside information was not available from research librarians, business analysts, or anyone else outside the inner circle at the targeted firm. Those secrets could only be obtained by spying.

Irving never used the term, "spy," of course, and seldom asked his agents to take more than minimal risks, more to protect himself than the agents. His methods were subtle, but very effective.

He understood "espionage by exposure," which was always easier to force on people than other, more obvious forms of spying. Someone who couldn't be forced into first-hand spying could often be talked into getting involved at one remove, once they were convinced that this was the only way they could save themselves. Irving was very convincing. He used videotapes, wire taps, and legal half-truths to beat his agents into submission.

Espionage by exposure required only that a person Irving controlled leave business secrets or other valuable information exposed where it could be accessed and copied by Ramsey. Secrets could be left "by accident" in a laptop computer at one of the back tables in the downtown library, copied by Ramsey, and the laptop retrieved by the owner, all in a matter of minutes.

Photos, blueprints and drawings could be intentionally left exposed near a window to be copied by Ramsey, by digiscoping.

Secrets could be purposely left unattended on computer screens, or read over someone's shoulder.

E-mail, faxes and other forms of electronic communications could be exposed and copied.

Espionage by exposure did not involve burglaries or the theft of equipment. There were no police reports to be filed or other red flags to attract attention. People do sometimes forget to lock things up, close window drapes, turn off computers. Accidents do happen. Espionage by exposure is so difficult to prove that even the government with all of its resources seldom gets convictions in such cases.

Espionage by exposure was only part of the game. Irving Cordell was also good at discovering derivative secrets and other spin-offs of the original information. These spin-offs often outnumbered the original secrets, sometimes by a factor of ten to one. He did database searches using the names of key people in the targeted firm, their important suppliers, and other outside contacts. He used several Internet identities, each to support the others in carefully targeted pretext attacks. These searches often revealed that key employees and contacts of the targeted firms gave interviews, wrote articles and took part in research projects their employers knew nothing about. These were all good sources of derivative secrets and new human targets.

Confidential business relationships were of special interest. He charted these complex connections using genealogy software to diagram the players. Many financial relationships, particularly those in international commerce, were not apparent until they were diagramed by computer. He used these data to develop Enterprise Profiles on targeted companies as part of his work for his clients, and People Profiles for his own use. He had learned early on that you don't have to be an insider to learn a secret; you just need a hook in an insider.

Irving Cordell sat in his modest office in the South tower of a block-square business complex downtown, and looked at his watch.

Espionage was a lucrative business, but there were some problems, primarily with personnel. As with most businesses, good help was hard to find. He needed a reliable working partner with a wide range of specialized skills, but most private eyes were either Internet junkies who did nothing but search the databases, or field men who didn't report in when they should and were off doing God knows what. Ramsey had become one of the latter.

Ramsey, Irving's current field man, was a good buggist, but suitable only as a private contractor, not as a business partner. He was even beginning to have doubts about the man's fieldwork. Ramsey got results on most assignments, but didn't stay in touch, and wasn't telling him everything that was going on, he was sure of that. He didn't completely trust Ramsey, but had been able to control him, at least up to this point, because he understood his weaknesses.

Ramsey was a fanatic, and like most fanatics, he believed in conspiracy theories because they provided easy answers for life's complex problems. To control him you had to provide these easy answers, and push the right buttons. Ramsey saw himself as a new-age spy, so you had to run him like a spy to feed his ego. He probably told women he met in bars that he worked for one of the government alphabet agencies. He needed a way to feel superior, needed a cause that would give him status, and needed someone to sanction his activities in the field.

As an attorney Irving supplied legal sanctions of sorts, at least Ramsey thought he did. That was fine as long as Ramsey stayed in line. Now things were different. He was sure Ramsey wasn't reporting everything he did on an assignment, and had started carrying a gun. Ramsey had a permit to carry the weapon, but most private eyes didn't carry, and anyway, why start now? A bad sign as far as he was concerned.

Irving looked at his watch again.

He was going to have it out with Ramsey, but the private eye wasn't due at the other office for almost an hour, so he had time to clear his desk. He needed to work on an overdue report.

Irving hated writing reports, but he couldn't trust it to anyone else since most of what he did was confidential. He had developed some basic guidelines to help simplify the report writing process.

He began with an overview of the operation.

After you have identified the executives and researchers who know the secrets you want and the security people who guard them, competitor intelligence is as easy as ABC.

A. First do surveillance to identify targets and to get a general idea of their daily activities.

B. Then do surveillance setups at selected locations to gather useful information, including the target's relationships with other people of interest. Use audio/video equipment to monitor negotiations in offices and boardrooms, then in more personal settings after the negotiations. Don't mention technical surveillance in the reports to clients. Give the impression that public records and other open sources were used throughout.

C. Fill out Enterprise Profile Forms for the client, but don't reveal the exploitable relationships you have developed as you may want to use them again later.

Make full use of the data gathered from public records and other open sources. Use these legitimate resources as a smokescreen to hide your clandestine activities.

Reveal as many of the target's informational assets as the operation warrants, but don't give anything away for free, and always suggest further work.

Use the following guidelines to write the report itself:

1. Always maintain direct control of the operation by acting as the handling official. Only the handling official is to know

the names of the clients, and how to contact them.

2. Write the reports in the third person to hide the identities of the clients, the operatives and the informants. Operatives and informants are referred to only by the numbers assigned to them by the handling official.

3. Sanitize all confidential reports going to the client. A pretext interview conducted by a field man should be reported as, "*Number xxx was overheard in conversation with...*" A wiretap should be reported as, "*Confidential Informant Number xxx reports...*"

4. All digital photographs and other images should be cropped to leave out any identifying material not directly related to the assignment, and not billable to the client.

5. Reports should be delivered in a secure manner, as specified by the client. Field men and other messengers should always be kept at a minimum of one remove. The confidentiality of both the firm and the client must be maintained at all costs.

Irving looked at his watch, then put the folder he had been working on back in the safe, spun the dials, and set the alarms. It was time to meet Ramsey at the other office.

Irving had the hall to himself as he left the small private office in the South tower where he did most of his work, and locked the doors behind him. The only people still in the towers at this time of night were the workaholics, the cleaning people, and a few security guards.

He went down four floors and across the sky bridge to the North tower and his other office. This second, more luxurious office was under a different name, on a different level, and a block away from the first, diagonally across the two buildings. He could walk there without going out on the street, an important advantage, especially at night. Three-dimensional movement was also more difficult for opponents to follow, just as it is in three-dimensional chess.

Irving thought of this second office as his "front" office, a little play on words. It had been professionally decorated in a style critics called attorney leather with a large v-shaped desk, deep leather chairs, and leather-topped side tables. The only things missing were the traditional shelves of leather-bound law books. The three fine oil paintings of falcons in flight among the glass towers of the business district were a reflection of his financial contributions to the City Bird Research Project.

The front office was large, luxurious and impressive, as it was meant to be. It made clients feel important and put subordinates in their place on those rare occasions when they were summoned to this inner sanctum. He had summoned Ramsey to the front office because he knew Ramsey hated being ordered around, especially to a meeting on someone else's turf, and because Ramsey needed to be taken down a peg.

Irving phoned to make sure that Ramsey was waiting at the security kiosk in the lobby of the North tower, then went to the mezzanine where he could look down on Ramsey without being seen. He always looked people over before he had them escorted up to the front office.

He watched while Ramsey methodically leafed through the local newspapers available in the machines in the lobby. He went through them page by page, but ignored the national publications. He was obviously looking for something local, but Irving had no idea what he was looking for.

Ramsey then went over to the security kiosk and turned on the guard's small portable TV. The guard gave him a dirty look and said something, but Ramsey had his jacket open as he leaned over to flip the dial. The guard saw Ramsey's pistol, probably thought he was a cop, and shut up.

Ramsey watched the headline news on each of the local stations, flipping from one to the other. Again, he was obviously looking for something specific. Ramsey was up to something or worried about something that wasn't reflected in his reports. Another bad sign, along with the pistol and not reporting in when he should.

Irving went back upstairs to the front office and checked the hidden security cameras. The cameras were monitored by the alarm company that installed them and included two-way audio communications and a panic button. He used the audio connection to talk with the night supervisor at the alarm company and then had Ramsey escorted up. He was tempted to have Ramsey check his pistol at the security kiosk in the lobby, but doubted that Ramsey would give up his gun to a security guard, or that the lobby guard could enforce the request.

Ramsey tried to take charge as soon as he walked into the front office and the security guard walked out.

He said, "What the fuck is this all about? What's so important it can't be handled by phone, or at one of our usual meeting places?"

Irving looked at the ornate grandfather's clock on the wall behind Ramsey, a useful interrogation tool placed there on purpose. He said nothing and waited to see what Ramsey would volunteer. Most people who are confronted with silence in an impressive setting become talkative despite themselves. Professional interrogators call this phenomenon "diarrhea of the mouth."

Ramsey was wise to the technique. All it did was piss him off.

"What the hell's going on? I thought we were supposed to keep our business confidential. I brought the latest tapes like you ordered, but I didn't expect you to have me bring them here. You've heard my verbal reports; why didn't you just have me drop off the tapes at one of the usual places? It's a whole lot safer."

Irving stared at the grandfather's clock behind Ramsey for several more seconds. Staring at the clock focused his eyes beyond the person standing in front of his desk, another interrogation technique which most people find disconcerting. Staring also helped keep his face impassive.

After a few more seconds he said, "Yes, I've heard your verbal reports and they're fine, as far as they go. The tapes you've turned in so far are fine too. I'm concerned with what you're not reporting, what you've left out."

"What do you mean? Are you accusing me of something?"

"We'll get to that after I've looked at this batch of tapes."

Irving took the tapes from Ramsey and fed the first one into a tape deck concealed in the bottom drawer of his desk, a deep file drawer that never held files. He could see the monitor also concealed in the drawer, but Ramsey couldn't.

Irving plugged in the headphones and began reviewing the tapes. He kept a straight face and watched Ramsey out of the corner of his eye. The tapes contained composite feeds from several video cameras, four of which could be displayed on the monitor at the same time or selectively displayed full-size one at a time. Audio was available when a picture was displayed full-size.

Irving watched the tapes for a few minutes, pushed buttons, and took notes. This was more for effect than anything else. He wanted to give the impression that something was wrong with Ramsey's work. As with all interrogations, including those called "interviews," it was a battle of nerves. He kept watching Ramsey out of the corner of his eye, and Ramsey blinked first.

Ramsey said, "What's the big deal? This batch is nothing special. It's all routine stuff."

"That's right, and that's one of the problems. You've spent a lot of time at the financial center lately, but all I'm seeing is routine stuff, at least on the tapes you turn in. You used to be more productive. What's going on?"

"I'm just being careful. Spying is dangerous work."

Irving said, "You mean gathering competitor intelligence on behalf of a client. The clients don't like the word 'spy', so we don't use it. Why do I have to keep reminding you of that?"

"I'm tired of all this double-talk! I call it spying because that's what it is. The clients want the inside info we feed them, but the 's' word leaves a shitty taste in their mouths. So what? You're a lawyer, you have to kiss up to the clients, but I don't. I'm a free agent, I tell it like it is."

"Okay, then tell me what's going on. What is it that you're not putting in your reports and that doesn't show up on the tapes? What are you looking for in the local papers and on TV? Why have you started carrying a gun? Go ahead, tell it like it is!"

"That's none of your business! It has nothing to do with you."

"Why don't you report in on time? That's my business and will be as long as you work for me."

"I've been busy. I can't always call in on schedule. I run an electronics business, make all the bugs I use and do all the fieldwork. All the important stuff. I know more about this business than you do because I do most of the work. I'm beginning to wonder what I need you for. You should think about that instead of poking your nose in my private affairs."

Irving thought, you're still being evasive, and now you're making veiled threats. I won't put up with that! Once the threats start in a relationship there's no turning back. You're on your way out as of now, but I need to know what you're up to before I fire your ass.

Irving held up both hands and smiled, his first agreeable gestures. He wanted to keep Ramsey talking long enough to tie up the loose ends. If he kept Ramsey talking, the truth or at least Ramsey's version of the truth, would eventually come out. He smiled again and nodded. "You may be right. You probably do know the business as well as I do, at least the technical part. I've never doubted that. I just thought you might be having some personal problems or something else I could help you with. I think we should talk about it."

Ramsey took this as an apology—a half-assed one, but as close to one as he'd get from a lawyer. He was relieved because Irving obviously didn't know about the kid on the ledge at the financial center, or the witch in the SUV. They weren't really a problem, but people who sat behind desks sometimes got cold feet when faced with the realities of field operations. As long as Irving didn't know what was going on and stayed out of his way, he could put up with the bastard a while longer. But once he got his hands on the client list, it was goodbye lawyer.

Ramsey said, "I've got no problems. I'm just busy. I've designed some surveillance equipment for one of my government clients and they've doubled up on the order."

Irving doubted that this was true, but went along with the story to keep Ramsey talking. He picked the first agency that came to mind.

"That's right, you did mention some work for the government. I think you said the ATF."

Ramsey had made up several stories about government work, but was a good liar and never allowed himself to be pinned down.

"The ATF? You got that wrong. What group of government assholes started an agency named the ATF? What were they thinking? Alcohol, Tobacco and Firearms, the three things the good old boys like best. That's got to be asking for trouble. A good old boy's favorite picture isn't of some naked broad he'd like to hump, it's a picture of himself with a jar of illegal whisky in one hand, an automatic weapon in the other, and a Cuban cigar in his mouth. The ATF is trying to control the good old boys's favorite pastimes. It was fucked from the start."

Irving laughed at Ramsey's joke. He'd seen the relief on Ramsey's face when he'd stopped asking questions about the financial center, so he knew he'd been on to something. Now Ramsey was telling jokes, another sign that he felt he was off the hook. This was going better than he had expected.

Irving got up from his desk, went over to the inside wall, and slid back an oak panel. A light went on in the mirrored alcove behind the panel revealing a wet bar, a colorful display of liquor bottles from around the world, and a dazzling display of crystal.

He turned his back on Ramsey, poured himself a shot glass of something, and drank it in one gulp. Then he had another one.

Ramsey said, "You drink that stuff like you need it."

Irving said, "I always have a few drinks at the end of the day. What can I get for you? We always keep the bar well-stocked."

"Who's the 'we'? Do you have another partner I don't know about? Maybe you're the one who's hiding something."

Irving thought, Good, now you're trying to question me. You probably think you've got me on the run. Just keep talking, you son-of-a-bitch, while I pick your brains.

Irving said, "No, I don't have another partner, but maybe we do need another man to help expand the business. Let me pour you a drink and let's talk about it."

Irving put the shot glass in the copper sink and poured himself a double brandy in a large snifter. He held the snifter in both hands as one would hold the face of a beloved child.

Ramsey watched what he thought was a man who drank too much, and would probably talk too much as the liquor took effect. He watched Irving work on the double brandy and decided to have a drink himself to keep Irving talking.

Ramsey said, "Thanks. I will have a drink, but I'll pour my own. I want to see what you've got."

He went to the bar and looked for an expensive Scotch whiskey in a bottle that hadn't been opened. When he found one he broke the seal and made himself a short drink with lots of ice.

Irving had a bad moment when Ramsey used the ice dispenser by the sink, but he didn't notice the oily shot glass or the few drops of oil that still remained in the bottom. Irving always coated his stomach with two shots of olive oil before he drank with someone he didn't trust. He wasn't a drunk, but sometimes acted like one if it was to his advantage.

They settled back in two of the deep leather chairs, drinks in hand, and grinned at each other. The battle lines were drawn. More throats have been cut over drinks in civilized settings than in back alleys.

Irving started off easy.

He said, "What do you think of Ian Scott? Would he make a good business partner?"

"A partner? You've got to be kidding! He's an asshole, and pussy whipped as well. The women run his class."

Irving laughed. "I take it you didn't enjoy Spy School at the zoo."

"I didn't learn anything new and didn't expect to. I always wondered why you had me take the class."

"I wanted to know if Ian Scott is in the same business we are. I like to keep track of the competition."

"That makes sense, but you should have told me up front so I'd know what to look for. The class itself was a waste of time."

"I wanted your reports to be objective."

"Well, 'Wildlife Surveillance with Camera & Recorder' sure as hell sounds suspicious, and birding is good cover for lots of things."

Irving said, "So what do you think? Is he a competitor or not? Your reports don't make that clear."

"He might be a competitor, but I doubt it. Anyway, he isn't street-wise enough to be a threat to us. He's more of a paper pusher. He's not in my league at least, that's for sure."

"What about the students in his class? Is there anyone you think might be working for him as an agent? Someone he's running?"

"Not that I know of. You saw the surveillance tapes I took of the class. They just look like a bunch of birders, mostly broads."

"Do you know if he has friends in our line of work?"

"He's friends with some old granny he knew in the Army. She's a volunteer with a shorebird project. That's about it. Most of the students are regular birders, but they do have some interesting high-tech equipment."

Irving said, "Like what?"

"High-end binoculars, scopes and cameras. Sensitive audio and video recording equipment for bird sights and sounds. Night vision equipment for owl prowls. Miniature cameras for watching what's going on inside nest boxes. Tracking devices that can be attached to falcons and other birds. You know. It's all in the reports."

Irving thought, yes, I know, you dumb bastard. This is the verification stage of the interrogation. I'm checking what you say now against what you've told me before. I want to tie up as many loose ends as I can before I kick your ass out of my office.

Irving said, "That sounds like the equipment you use."

"More or less, only my electronics are better. Like I told you, I make my own stuff."

"So Ian Scott could be a competitor, but you're not sure. He and his students have equipment and skills that could be used in competitor intelligence gathering, but you're not sure about that either. Is that it? That's not much to go on. Is there anything you do know for sure—*for sure?*"

"I know Ian Scott's not going to be your new partner. I can guarantee that!"

Irving looked dazed, but wasn't. He went back to the alcove to refill his brandy snifter, this time from an identical bottle filled with tea. He had intentionally spilled a little of the brandy on his necktie to retain the scent of the liquor.

Ramsey had watched Irving drink two straight shots, sip double brandies, and now go back for more. The lawyer was becoming belligerent, so he must be getting drunk. It was time to move in for the kill.

Ramsey stood up and let his coat swing open. He said, "I'm tired of being treated like hired help. There's going to be some changes in how this business is run, starting now. To begin with, I want to know who I'm working for. I can guess, but I want to know for sure. I want a list of the clients. You're just a go-between, as far as I'm concerned."

Irving still looked dazed, as if he didn't know what was going on. He was acting confused to see what would happen, an interrogation technique that works well when the subject thinks he has the upper hand.

Irving said, "Changes in the business? You mean the business at the financial center? You already run that operation pretty much on your own. What do you want to change? Are there some problems?"

Ramsey looked surprised, opened his mouth to say something but didn't follow through. He stood silent for a moment as Irving got to his feet and moved toward the bar.

Irving thought, I am onto something! The bastard lies or freezes up whenever I mention the financial center. The son-of-a-bitch is in some kind of trouble and it can only get worse. I'd better finish this and get him out of here before whatever it is rubs off on me.

Irving moved away from the bar and sat down at his desk. He decided to make one more try and then drop it.

He said, "Are there still some loose ends at the financial center? Something involving the listening post, or the Fool's Phone in the lobby? Is that what you mean?"

Ramsey got red in the face, walked to the desk, leaned across and slammed his hands flat on the polished surface.

He said, "Forget the fucking financial center! I'm talking about this business. The spy business. I'm your new partner, whether you like it or not. Can't you get that through your head? You've probably covered your ass, got me set up to take a fall if I make trouble, but that won't mean shit if you're not around to make it happen. You got that?"

Ramsey pushed his coat back to expose the pistol, an obvious threat impossible to ignore.

Irving thought, this has gone too far! Now he's threatening me with a gun in my own office!

As an attorney Irving often used words as weapons, but he knew that words were a poor defense against an angry man with a gun. He tried to stare Ramsey down, but had lost control of the interrogation, and this time he blinked first.

Strange what runs through your mind when you're frightened. Irving recalled an old joke where a lawyer and his assistant were walking through the woods when attacked by a bear. The lawyer kicked the assistant in the knee, and ran for it. The lawyer knew he didn't have to outrun the bear, he just had to outrun his assistant.

Irving pushed the panic button under the edge of his desk. The hidden security cameras were monitored by the alarm company that installed them, and included two-way audio communications activated by the panic button. The voice of the night supervisor at the alarm company came through loud and clear.

"Can I help you, sir? Is there a problem?"

Irving said, "Is the system working? Can you see what's going on here in my office?"

"Yes, sir, we cover your entire office and, as always, we began videotaping when you pressed the button. I say again, is there a problem?"

Irving remembered the recognition word he had selected to signal that he wasn't being held against his will. He used his mother's pet name from college, a name he remembered well since he still used it in his letters to her, of which he kept copies. He said, "Buffy says everything's fine for now, but I want you to keep videotaping this conversation. I'm terminating this employee and I want a record of the proceedings."

Ramsey said, "You bastard! You'll live to regret this!"

Irving spoke to the grandfather's clock behind Ramsey.

"Don't make threats. You'd better leave before you get yourself in trouble. The security cameras will track you out of the office, and out of the building. Anything you say or do becomes part of the record."

Ramsey said, "You and that asshole Ian Scott are already hooked up, aren't you? That's the only way this makes sense. You wouldn't fire me unless you had him lined up to do the field work!"

"Please leave."

"Oh, I'll leave all right, but this isn't over, for you or for Scott."

The alarm company's night supervisor was a retired Army sergeant who knew when to raise his voice.

He said, "Do you want us to escort this man out of the building or call the police and have them do it?"

Irving wasn't sure what Ramsey would do if someone tried to physically throw him out of the building, or worse yet, tried to disarm him. Ramsey wasn't one of the gray-haired, gunpowder-equals-Viagra crowd who think that being disarmed is having your balls cut off, but who knew at what age that started? The last thing he wanted was an armed confrontation that was sure to attract the media.

Irving said, "Let the man leave on his own. Don't call the police unless he causes problems."

Ramsey buttoned his coat and headed for the door. He didn't know where the security cameras were hidden, but took a chance on his way out. He ducked behind the office door, pointed his index finger back at Irving Cordell, and cocked his thumb.

Irving had a double brandy, a real one, when he was sure Ramsey was out of the building.

Chapter 8
Odd Birds

Ian Scott was having a breakfast bowl of plain rolled oats and honey prepared by pouring boiling water over the oats just as they came from the familiar round cardboard box. He was eating his one-bowl breakfast over the kitchen sink as he listened to the morning news on the radio and watched the backyard birds outside the kitchen window.

A chickadee, America's favorite backyard bird, was zipping in and out of a lilac bush as it took black sunflower seeds from the tube feeder under the eaves and returned to the bush to eat them. The lilac bush needed pruning and the grass in the backyard needed cutting, but the small bungalow he was house-sitting was slightly rundown, and so was at home with its surroundings.

Ian was watching the chickadee peck open a sunflower seed when the phone rang. His calls were being forwarded from a business phone in another city, so he turned off the radio to keep the background mix of local news and advertisements from providing clues to his present location. He favored one-word greetings that didn't reveal his name, the telephone number, or if it was morning or evening at his present location, until he knew who was calling. He saw no need to be negative, however.

"Yes?"

"This is Maggie Warren."

"I recognize your voice, but this isn't the best connection. Where are you?"

"I'm driving north up the freeway to Skagit Valley. Adrian's supposed to be up there running around with some falconers. I have their cell phone number, but I haven't been able to get through to them so far. The cell phone service is lousy, but I should get a stronger signal as I get closer. I know about where he is so I'm going there in person to run him down. I'll give that kid hell when I get my hands on him!"

Maggie seemed relieved by the news concerning her grandson.

Ian said, "Are you sure he's up there?"

"I think so. The girl I talked to on the phone lives in Bow near the wildlife reserve. She says she saw Adrian near there two days ago. She knows Adrian by sight, but she doesn't know the guys he's with. I suppose I shouldn't be surprised, Adrian's always into something new."

"Are these registered falconers? If so, they shouldn't be hard to find."

Maggie said, "I'm not sure, and I know what you're thinking. If Adrian is running around with some of the people on the fringes of falconry it would explain why he's being so secretive. That kid! If he's doing something illegal, I'll kick his butt!"

"If he's interested in falcons, the Skagit Flats is the place to be. All five North American species show up there at one time or another."

"Yes, I know."

Ian said, "Good luck. I hope you find him without too much trouble."

"Hey wait, don't hang up on me. I called you, remember? Have you talked to Laura this morning?"

"No, why?"

"She called me a few minutes ago with what she thinks is a new address for Adrian, a place I've never heard of. I told her I was headed to Skagit Valley, and the rest of what I just told you. Can I get you to follow up on this with her?"

Ian said, "Are you playing matchmaker?"

"I wouldn't wish you on any woman, but Laura went out of her way to help me find Adrian, so I'd appreciate it if you'd follow through on this. It's probably nothing, but if Adrian is into something illegal I want to know about it. Give her a call, okay? It will do you good to talk with an intelligent woman who's wise to your wicked ways."

"I don't think Laura likes me very much."

"I told you she was intelligent! She's not one of the odd birds you usually connect with in your travels."

"What odd birds?"

"You know what I mean. You don't go to bars or cruise the clubs or play the classified ads like some of the guys. You go out of your way to meet strange women in strange places. That makes you an odd bird yourself, in case you haven't noticed. Your friends sure have!"

"Thank you for sharing that critique of my personal life. It's just what I need first thing in the morning."

"You're welcome. You'll call Laura? She's at the zoo."

"Yes, I guess that's the least I can do. I'll keep you posted."

After Maggie hung up, Ian rinsed his breakfast bowl under

the tap in the kitchen sink and went to the old-fashioned pantry that had been converted into a small office. As he checked his e-mail he wondered what Maggie had been trying to tell him. Friends were supposed to tell you what you needed to hear, but Maggie was an old soldier and her remarks weren't always what one might expect from a soft-spoken grandmother.

Maggie had been wrong about one thing. He didn't go out of his way to meet strange women. If he was lucky enough to meet an interesting woman it was while he was living his life and going about his business. He used a technique field agents use to get close to persons of interest, but no one could control what happened in their personal life, and he didn't wish to. That was one of the things that made it exciting. People are always looking for ways to meet each other. Most eventually find a way that works for them, at least part of the time. No matter how crude an approach may seem, if the person using it is an adult, that approach has probably worked before with someone else or it wouldn't still be in use.

Ian had been taught a technique called "one-step-further." The instructor had been a woman, but the approach worked for both sexes. He used it because it was a benign, non-threatening approach that worked well in many everyday situations. Interesting people were where you found them, which could be anywhere.

Odd things about women attracted his attention: a woman in a designer suit going into an alley in the business district at five in the morning to give a bag lady money, an artist making crude sketches in a museum, a woman blacksmith with the tip of a finger missing, or Laura building a bird habitat at the zoo.

Curiosity was the motivator. Who was the dressy woman in the designer suit, and why was she in the business district at five in the morning? Was the woman in the museum really an artist, despite the crudeness of her sketches? Why would a woman do the hot, dirty work of a blacksmith? And, of course, who was Laura, and why was an English woman working at a zoo in the U.S.?

Curiosity was supposed to kill the cat, but in his case, the cat kept smiling.

Ian would smile at an interesting woman wherever he found her. If she smiled in return he would say something appropriate to begin a casual conversation. If the woman stopped to talk he would go one step further and suggest coffee or cocktails. If the two of them seemed compatible he'd suggest something more, or the woman would.

He never went more than one step further so that the woman didn't feel pressured. If she resisted his approach, he would smile and excuse himself, then back away. An interesting woman could often be approached again later when their paths crossed, since he wasn't overly aggressive at any point in the step-by-step process.

There were no guarantees, of course. Laura wouldn't even give him her home address, a symbolic gesture since she knew very well he could get it by other means. He wouldn't, of course. To quote his mentor: "It just isn't done. It isn't seemly."

Ian finished his e-mail, locked that laptop in the firearms safe built into a closet, and took out another. He owned three identical laptops, each dedicated to a different purpose. He also had several cameras he used for different purposes, including a small digital camera he carried with him as a personal photo notebook. Farmer's daughters weren't the only ones wise enough not to keep all their eggs in one basket.

His call to Laura at the zoo was transferred to the extension phone at her worksite. He recognized her voice, but the call didn't start off very well, and it didn't get any better.

"This is Ian Scott. Maggie told me to call you."

"Was that an order? I wouldn't want to put you out."

"I'm sorry, I didn't mean it that way. We always seem to get off on the wrong foot. I'm happy to hear your voice; in fact, I'd like to…"

"Oh, shit, he's here again."

"Who is?"

"Ramsey, that sleazy private eye."

"Where are you?"

"I'm in the new outdoor exhibit I'm working on at the aviary. He's inside in the gallery, where he was before."

"What's he doing?"

"Watching the spot near the stone wall outside the enclosure."

"Has he seen you?"

"I don't think so."

"Do you feel threatened?"

"No, but this guy gives me the creeps."

"Stay where you are. I'll be there in a few minutes."

As he drove to the zoo, Ian remembered that the aviary was built around a central gallery. The glass-fronted exhibits faced inward and featured natural settings. Most of the exhibits were completely enclosed and climate-controlled to accommodate tropical birds, but the exhibit Laura was working on was for native birds that were used to the local weather conditions. Her exhibit extended from the inside viewing area through to an outside enclosure to give the native birds more room, and the viewers more options.

Laura had led Ian along the gallery to a point where they could look through from the inside exhibit to the outside enclosure. She'd seen Ramsey hide something outside near the stone wall where an Asian man in a hooded sweatshirt had picked it up later. Ramsey had watched the man make the pick-up from the inside gallery, but hadn't tried to follow him. Ian had thought at the time that probably meant Ramsey already knew where the man was going.

This time when Ian reached the zoo, Laura was waiting for him near the security booth at the zoo entrance. He had told her to stay where she was but knew she would make her own decisions, depending on the circumstances. She waved to him as he came through the gate.

Laura had tears in her eyes.

She said, "April just called. May was killed in a car accident last night on her way home after your class. They were scheduled to work with me for a few hours today as volunteers, so April called to tell me what happened. Poor kid, she's taking it hard, as you can imagine."

"What happened?"

"May apparently ran off the road on that street that winds down the hill to their apartment on the lake."

Ian took Laura's hand.

"I'm sorry. I didn't know May very well. I don't even know her real name, but I know that you two worked together."

"She was a good person."

"Do you know what time it happened?"

"No. Late, I think. April was worried about her and had tried to call her several times. She thinks May was following Ramsey in her car after their argument in class. May had tried to follow him before when he and April were dating, but could never keep up with him. May never trusted Ramsey!"

"May was following Ramsey after class and then ran off the road?"

"That's what she said. April was crying and I couldn't hear all of it."

"And now Ramsey's here, at the zoo?"

"Yes, at least he was a few minutes ago."

Ian said, "Where was he when you last saw him?"

"He was watching the people near the outside exhibit at the aviary, then took off walking around the grounds."

"Which way was he headed?"

"He was walking east toward the outdoor animal exhibits."

"Do you feel safe here?"

"I'm fine. I'll go back to my office in a few minutes."

"Good. I'll meet you there."

"What are you going to do?"

"I'm going to talk with Ramsey, if I can find him."

"You think he had something to do with what happened to May?"

"I don't know. He threatened her in class and she died a few hours later. I'd like to know where he was at that time."

Laura still had tears in her eyes, but had only her keys and her cell phone with her. Ian patted her hand and gave her one of the big white handkerchiefs he carried with him in the field. She tried to smile, then took a step toward him and kissed him on the cheek. The kiss was so unexpected that he couldn't think what to say as she turned and went into the security booth.

Ian walked east toward the outdoor animal exhibits.

He knew the grounds well. Some of his former students had gone gaming after class, playing the spy game by secretly photographing those who visited the zoo. The person who took the best pictures of unsuspecting subjects in the allotted time won the game. The rules were simple and intimate pictures of young lovers, in any combination, were sure winners.

Ian had put a stop to that by turning the tables. His photos of the gamers themselves as unsuspecting subjects had put their game in a new light, especially when they saw the prurient looks on their own faces as they were caught taking intimate photos of other people. After that, most of the gamers had second thoughts about what they were doing and the others—the hardcore voyeurs—took their spy game somewhere else.

Ian's game within a game with his students had taken him to many places on the grounds. He knew the best vantage points to see without being seen, and now used this knowledge to track Ramsey.

It was still morning. There weren't as many people around the animal exhibits as there would be later in the day, but it still took some time to check all of the likely spots. He had covered the other enclosures without success when he reached the elephant house at the lower end of the park. Ramsey wasn't there either, but as Ian left he caught a glimpse of him crossing the old concrete footbridge that led through a wooded area to the lower parking lot.

Ramsey stopped among the trees at a spot where he could look back at the footbridge without being seen, took out a digital camera and began playing tourist.

There was no way Ian could cross the footbridge or the busy street below without being seen. He stayed on his own side of the street, but moved away from the elephant house to a vantage point where he could see into the lower parking lot. He carried his own small digital camera as a personal photo notebook.

Ramsey watched the footbridge for several minutes to see if he was being followed, then walked through the trees toward the lower parking lot. The parking lot served the lawn bowling green, but there weren't any bowlers there at that hour. There was only one car in the parking lot.

A small Asian man in a sweat suit was waiting in a Honda.

When Ramsey appeared through the trees he got out of the car with a colorful city map in his left hand. It must have been a recognition signal, since Ramsey took out a map of the same color from a side pocket.

Ian took pictures from his side of the highway. He didn't expect to get it all without a long lens, but he could see that the Asian wasn't happy. The man kept his right hand inside his sweatshirt and talked fast. He waved Ramsey away with the map as he spoke, but Ramsey was talking fast also, and kept moving closer. It was obvious that the Asian didn't know Ramsey, and didn't want to. He was warning Ramsey off with gestures, and apparently with words.

Ramsey kept talking and the Asian kept shaking his head. Ramsey had his jacket open to reveal the pistol tucked in his belt, but the Asian wasn't intimidated. He was light on his feet as he stepped to Ramsey's right in the bent-kneed stance of someone trained in the martial arts.

Ramsey was trying to force the issue. He apparently wanted in on something but the Asian wouldn't even talk about it. If he was a go-between, he obviously had orders that Ramsey was to go no farther. His answer to everything Ramsey said was a sharp shake of the head, but he never took his eyes off Ramsey. Ian could see his facial expression each time his mouth formed the word, "No!" He kept waving Ramsey off with the map the way one would shoo a troublesome dog away at a picnic.

Ramsey put his hand on his belt near his pistol. The Asian had a small pistol in his right hand when he took his hand out of his sweatshirt. He pointed it in Ramsey's general direction. They both stopped talking and stared at each other.

Experts know that the traditional Asian martial arts are good exercises for mind and body, but *Hojutsu*, the way of the gun, is the relevant martial art for this millennium.

The Asian knew he probably couldn't stop Ramsey with the first shot from his small pistol, especially if Ramsey was wearing body armor. Ramsey knew his heavy revolver would stop the Asian, but didn't know if he could hit the smaller man with his first shot, and knew he might not have time for another.

Ramsey backed away, spat on the ground, and walked toward the footbridge. The Asian got back in the Honda and drove away.

Ian lost track of Ramsey in the trees near the footbridge. When he found him again, Ramsey was still on the other side of the busy street scanning the hillside near Ian through the viewfinder of his camera. Ian couldn't be sure how much Ramsey could see or at what magnification, so he stood perfectly still in what he hoped was a concealed position.

It became a battle of nerves, as is often the case during surveillance. Roles can quickly become reversed with the hidden watcher becoming the target if he loses his nerve and gives away his position.

Watchers always have questions when they think they've been spotted and Ian was no exception. How much could Ramsey see? Had he used his cell phone to call for some sort of backup? Was someone already working their way down the hill behind him? Was Ramsey worried enough, or crazy enough, to force a direct confrontation?

The pressure builds when you don't have answers.

Ian waited. Ramsey kept scanning the hillside on Ian's side of the footbridge and kept taking pictures. After a few minutes that seemed much longer, Ramsey finally gave way to the first of the family groups to cross the footbridge that morning. Ian watched him until he disappeared going east through the trees toward the lake and the other parking areas. He didn't try to follow. There were dozens of places where Ramsey could spot a foot surveillance and three miles of footpaths around the lake that led to other parking lots, bus stops, taxis, and even a place where he could rent a bicycle. Ramsey had a choice of many vantage points and many modes of transportation.

Watchers always have questions when they think they've been spotted. Ian's questions continued, even when the immediate threat appeared to be over. Had Ramsey seen him but decided that a confrontation at the zoo wasn't to his advantage? Would Ramsey target him later? If Ramsey hadn't seen him, could the digital photos he'd taken be processed, pixel-by-pixel, to reveal his presence? Ramsey knew him by sight so it wouldn't have to be a good picture. Ian used his own pocket digital camera as a personal photo notebook, and often used a computer program to enhance the photos.

Ian watched and waited for a few more minutes, then went back up the hill toward the aviary. There were still two more question, of course, two that had come up before and were behind all the others. *What was Ramsey up to? Why would a private eye act like a government spy?*

Ian used his cell phone to check in with his handling official. They didn't talk long and used a simple contract code to make general conversation.

When Ian had taken the assignment, his handling official had set up the contract code by jotting down random numbers next to the names of each key person, place and thing shown on the original case file. Any numbers would do, as long as each one was different. Ian had his list of the coded items disguised as a grocery list on a three-by-five card.

The short conversation with his handling official sounded like engineering jargon, but covered the who, what, where and when of his surveillance of Ramsey. Contract codes were not a substitute for encryption, but they didn't require the use of sophisticated equipment and have many low-tech applications. He didn't have much to report, in any case.

Ian's handling official had a perverted sense of humor and often signed off with, "Keep smiling." Ian didn't have much to smile about at the moment. He was a skeptic in a world where it was safer to be a cynic. Cynics didn't have to prove anything, of course; they'd already made up their minds. Skeptics searched for proof. This was hard work and often dangerous for the searcher.

Ian had always been good in the field, but was considered a pain in the ass at the agency office. Now all he had was part-time work as a field consultant, the best he could do under the circumstances. He had no idea what was going on behind the scenes, but hoped that he wasn't being hung out to dry.

His personal concerns temporarily took second place when he met Laura at her office. He told her he hadn't been able to catch up with Ramsey and she seemed relieved, but distracted. She was trying to get on with her work while taking time out to comfort April by phone, and trying to keep a stiff upper lip to go with her English heritage. She wasn't succeeding very well, and things were about to get worse.

They had hoped Maggie would find her grandson up in Skagit County. That hope disappeared with the vibration of Ian's cell phone.

"Yes?"

"This is Maggie."

"Did you find him?"

"No. It turns out the girl I talked with on the phone is a flake. I'm not sure she knows what day of the week it is. I tracked down the would-be falconers he was running around with up here and Adrian left the morning of the day he disappeared. I went to the sheriff's office to file a missing persons report, but I don't think it did much good. It's only been two days, three at the most, since he went missing and now I don't even know in which county."

Ian said, "Do you have any leads?"

"I think Adrian was looking for falcon chicks to raise as his own. The guys he was running around with wouldn't tell me much, but Adrian had bragged about working downtown at the financial center and they had seen the falcon chicks at the center on TV. They put two and two together."

"Anything I can do?"

"Yes. Do you have an address for Ramsey what's-his-name? There's nothing but a business service address in the phone book and I don't see him listed anywhere else."

"I don't have an address for him. He paid his class fees in cash and I don't require a home address. Why do you ask?"

Maggie said, "I'm beginning to think Ramsey knows something about Adrian's disappearance. They crossed paths several times when Adrian worked at the financial center, but he never knew for sure why Ramsey was there, and he was afraid of him. Adrian, Ramsey, falcon chicks and the financial center. If there isn't some connection it's one hell of a coincidence."

"You may be right, but stay away from Ramsey. He's a dangerous man."

Maggie said, "I'm an old soldier. I can take care of myself. You, of all people, should know that."

"That was a few years back."

Maggie's voice changed from soft-spoken grandmother to career Army.

She said, "I won't argue with you. This is family business and I look after my own."

"Do you still want my help?"

"Yes, of course, but don't tell me what to do. You do your thing and I'll do mine. Just keep in touch."

Maggie hung up and Laura's office phone rang a few seconds later. When she reached for it, Ian placed his hand on top of hers to keep her from picking up the receiver.

Ian said, "That's probably Maggie. She thinks Ramsey had something to do with Adrian's disappearance. She asked me for his address, which I don't have, and now she will probably want the new address you have for Adrian in hopes of finding new clues. I don't know where that will lead, but I don't want her tangling with Ramsey, so don't tell her any more than you have to."

Laura said, "I won't lie to her."

"Do you want her confronting Ramsey in some dark alley? We don't know what he's up to yet, but we both know he's a dangerous man."

Ian took his hand away from Laura's and waited while she made her decision. She picked up the phone on the next ring.

"This is Laura."

"Hi, this is Maggie. Is Ian there? I heard zoo noises in the background when I called him a few minutes ago. I figured he was either in your office or on the way."

"Yes, he's here."

"I'm looking for Adrian's new address. You said you knew something and I asked Ian to follow up on it with you. Have you checked it out?"

Laura said, "I know the district. I think it's Ballard, but I don't really have an address. It's an old gray house across the street from the ship canal. It shouldn't be too hard to find."

"Is that all you have or is Ian being protective? That man is a pain in the butt sometimes."

"That's all I know."

The two women spent a few minutes talking about the funeral arrangements April was making for May, but soon ran out of things to say, in part because Ian was in Laura's office. Ian knew Laura had lied to Maggie by the look on her face when she hung up the phone. When she told a fib as a child, her mother had always reminded her about the tangled web we weave when we practice to deceive. Now she was caught up in Ian's web and it was obvious from the expression on her face that she didn't like it. Ian answered her unasked question before she could voice her displeasure.

"You did the right thing. We can't stop Maggie from tracking Ramsey, but I might be able to find out what's happened to Adrian and clear this up before it gets out of hand. Tell me what you've learned and I'll look into it personally and keep you posted."

"Whatever you tell me I'll pass on to Maggie."

"I understand that."

"Well, as I said before, I saw Adrian at a meat market in the Fremont district a week ago. I was in a hurry, so I didn't stop to talk. He picked up several small packages wrapped in butcher paper and seemed to know the butcher. I thought it was odd at the time since young guys don't usually do much cooking, especially starting from scratch. So I went back to the butcher shop and sweet-talked the butcher. He told me Adrian bought cubed meat and said it was for his birds. He said Adrian lives in Fremont, within walking distance of the butcher shop, but that's all he knew."

"You told Maggie an old gray house across from the ship canal in Ballard."

"I lied."

"Thank you."

As Ian left to check out Laura's lead, he realized that he

hadn't thanked her for the kiss on the cheek, but had thanked her for lying.

What sort of man did that?

Chapter 9
Beauty, Nobility
and Death

Laura had said she thought Adrian lived in the Fremont district, within walking distance of the butcher shop. Directions like that sound simple until you look at a detailed map. "Within walking distance" covers a lot of ground because it goes in all four directions, plus up and down stairs and walkways on all levels. Field operatives know this and cringe when inexperienced handling officials assign neighborhood investigations without giving specific addresses. In this case, Ian was on his own and knew his injured foot would take a beating.

He had one piece of information that might narrow the search. Adrian had bought cubed meat and said it was for his birds. Knowing what he now knew about Adrian, that probably meant falcons, or at least raptors, though some other birds also ate meat.

Fremont was a good place for falcons, a better place than one might expect to find within the city limits. Good habitat and good hunting. There were pigeons and waterfowl along the ship canal and in the parks and open grasslands near the college. The habitat was enhanced by the freshwater lake at one end of the canal and the saltwater sound at the other. The area was gradually becoming gentrified but there were still some old houses for rent that attracted the younger crowd with less money.

Ian went to the boarding kennel to pick up Buster. The dog needed some time away from the kennel and a dog is excellent cover when canvassing a neighborhood. Birding is better cover, of course, but Buster needed a break and a chance to explore the great outdoors.

The little gray nondescript mutt had been part of someone else's cover story, abandoned when that story was no longer needed. People did that when a dog had outlived its usefulness, or when a cute puppy grew up to be ugly, or an old dog needed expensive care. Buster had been dumped at an animal shelter and ended up with the old, the ugly, and the unloved, out of sight at the back of the shelter in the area referred to as "death row." Ian thought Buster deserved better than that and had bailed him out at the last minute.

Buster wasn't much to look at, part two or three types of terrier, part who knew what. He had his good points, however. He was curious and intelligent with sharp eyes, keen hearing and an inquisitive nose, a useful combination when canvassing a neighborhood on foot in the daylight hours—a necessity if the investigation continued after dark. An extra pair of eyes and ears, and a sensitive nose, added a new and important dimension to a neighborhood walk, as Ian and millions of other dog owners learned by paying close attention to the actions of their animal companions.

Ian stopped at the kennel office to pay Buster's bills, then picked up the dog at the back door to the parking lot. Buster wasn't a wiggly hand-licker, but accepted a pat on the head and seemed glad to see him. Ian snapped a leash on his collar and let him stand up in the passenger's seat of the rental car so that he could look out the window.

When they got to the Fremont district, Ian removed Buster's collar, put on his harness and wiped the smell of the kennel off his face with a clean white handkerchief soaked in bottled distilled water. Buster lived by his nose, experiencing the world around him as a mixture of past olfactory events and ongoing odors. He liked having his face washed and pushed his muzzle into the wet cloth.

When they were finished with the face-washing ritual, Ian signaled that it was time to go to work by rinsing the handkerchief in bottled water, wringing it out and putting it into a plastic bag. Buster sat on the curb beside the open car door while Ian adjusted the elastic foot brace on his left foot and tightened his shoelaces, another part of the ritual.

They began working the neighborhood near the butcher shop, but didn't go back to talk with the butcher. If the butcher hadn't told all he knew to a pretty woman like Laura, it was unlikely he would have anything new to add at this point, especially to another stranger asking the same questions. He might even become suspicious and call a friend, or a friend of a friend, who could interfere with the investigation. Neighborhood people often gossip about their neighbors, but they also gossip about anyone from outside the neighborhood who is asking questions.

Ian and Buster started working the side streets. When they

began zigzagging in and out of the alleys around the old rental houses, Buster poked his nose into everything, but kept looking back at Ian as if to say, "What are we looking for?" Ian was glad Buster couldn't talk because he couldn't answer the question. The best he could say was, "Something to do with raptors."

Despite his bad foot, Ian was used to walking. Long walks had been part of most of his agency assignments, especially at the beginning. He walked to familiarize himself with his assigned areas and the available modes of public transportation, and to locate places for meetings and message drops. He looked for routes to and from these places that had twists and turns that would help him spot a surveillance.

He walked to lay the groundwork for future operations or just to confuse the opposition by forcing them to waste their time and resources trying to figure out what he was up to. Long walks could be useful both ways, as a means to one's own ends as a field operative and as a way of spotting the opposition. The opposition was doing the same thing, of course.

Neighborhood alleys were always of interest to dogs and other curious observers. Part private road, part service area, alleys revealed more about the occupants of a house than the street out front and the formal face the house revealed to the public. There were few secrets in alleys. Large numbers of empty liquor bottles lost in the garbage may reveal a heavy drinker; the same liquor bottles carefully wrapped in newspaper and hidden in garbage bags inside the can may suggest a secret drinker. Clues to everything that happened in a house with an alley ended up in the alley sooner or later, one way or another. Alleys were the ongoing archeological sites of our society.

Ian and Buster were an hour and a half into their walk when the dog earned his keep in one of the alleys by showing an interest in an unlocked refrigerator on the back porch of a rundown two-story house. Most refrigerators on back porches were locked and filled with beer and other items that wouldn't fit into the refrigerator in the kitchen. When Buster showed interest, Ian was also interested since Buster didn't drink beer. Buster ran up onto the porch, sniffed at the refrigerator and pawed at the door. The house looked deserted, so Ian walked up onto the porch to see what Buster had discovered.

The refrigerator wasn't plugged in and was being used as an icebox. The bag of ice inside had melted and an open package of meat scraps from the local butcher had begun to stink. A note stuck to the inside of the door said, "Adrian, it's your turn to clean the refer!"

Ian closed the refrigerator door and gave Buster a dog biscuit, a poor substitute for the meat in the refrigerator judging from Buster's reaction. Ian patted him on the head and walked him around the house as if looking for a way through to the street.

One of the side windows was curtained with a patterned bed sheet, white daisies on a yellow background. As with most curtained windows there was a small gap, enough for Ian to see into the living room. The room contained an old couch, two overstuffed chairs and a TV set so old it was hardly worth stealing. There was no one in the living room or in the hallway leading to the other first-floor rooms.

Ian watched Buster's reactions as they continued on around the house.

The dog gave no indication that anyone else was on the property. When they reached the back porch again, Ian knocked on the door, waited and listened for a full minute, then popped the door the way most burglars do, with a swift kick to the edge of the door near the lock. Given the circumstances, he saw no need to signal his level of expertise by picking the lock or carrying a set of lock picks.

The house smelled musty but lived in, a mixture of poor housekeeping and fast-food smells still lingering in pizza boxes and Styrofoam cartons in the garbage can under the sink. The sink itself had rings of rust around both faucets.

Ian stood still and let Buster's eyes, ears and nose do their work. Dogs were pack animals and would willingly assist their human pack members, given the chance. Ian stood with his back to the wall in the dingy hallway and used his limited human senses as best he could, but let Buster assume reconnaissance duty. Ian carried a small revolver for personal protection, but wasn't looking for a fight.

Buster worked the first floor of the house without reacting beyond what one would expect from a mixed-breed terrier. Some of his ancestors had been bred to hunt small ground-dwelling game, including the huge European rats few cats will tackle, but other hunting skills were also part of the mix. That was the marvel of mutts: the mix was often superior to its individual components.

Buster stopped at the foot of the stairs leading to the second floor, looked up and barked. The short sharp bark echoed throughout the house and made Ian flinch. When Ian moved to join him at the foot of the stairs, Buster stopped barking and Ian heard a faint thumping from behind the door on the upper landing.

Buster seemed more aggressive than frightened, but since he wasn't one of the large breeds bred for aggressive behavior, Ian took hold of his harness to keep him from running upstairs. With Ian's hand on his harness Buster went into stop, look and listen mode, a natural response to a command from his human pack leader.

Buster's bark would have alerted anyone in the house to

their presence, even if they hadn't heard Ian kick in the back door. They had lost the element of surprise, if they'd ever had it, so Ian did what seemed logical under the circumstances.

He called out, "Hello there. Anyone home? I'm looking for Adrian Warren. We're worried about him."

When no one answered, he let Buster lead the way upstairs.

Buster pawed at the upstairs door. The thumping sounds inside increased. When Ian opened the door, Buster ran across the room to two homemade cages facing a south window, jumped at the cages and barked again. Ian called him away and quieted him down while holding onto his harness.

A large red-tailed hawk was thumping its wings against the wire of one of the cages while a small American kestrel fluttered in the other. The two species were commonly used in the two-year training program for apprentice falconers, but no legitimate falconer would keep birds in these makeshift mews under these unhealthy conditions. The cages reeked with the smell of droppings and rotted meat, inches deep in some places. Falconry has been described as a sport of beauty, nobility and death, but there would be only death for these birds if they didn't receive professional care, and soon.

Ian covered the cages with the old blankets kept there for that purpose. This quieted both the birds and Buster. Ian turned to the room. The birds would have to wait a while longer for the care they deserved.

Ian had entered Adrian's secret world. He was also walking in dead man's shoes although he wasn't aware of that. He was aware of the smell, and the trash underfoot, as he viewed his surroundings.

The wall between the two upstairs bedrooms had been removed to convert the second floor to studio space in some previous remodel. The makeshift mews took up part of the south wall, the rest of the space was cluttered living quarters.

Ian began searching Adrian's secret world by starting in the area closest to the entrance. He used search techniques he had used so often that they were second nature.

First, the most obvious places: the hall table and the cork board near the door where people often post notes to remind themselves of appointments, keep incoming and outgoing mail, and sometimes leave keys for each other. A few outdated housekeeping notes stuck to the corkboard, indicating that at least two people shared these quarters—Adrian and someone who used the name "Cygnet"—but there was nothing of interest in the notes or on the hallway table.

Then the drawers. He opened the bottom drawer of each piece of furniture first, then worked his way up so that he didn't have to close the one above to see into the one below. He then closed all of the drawers at once to save time.

He looked carefully at everything, then put it back exactly where it was before. Why search a place and then leave clues that tell the occupants you have searched it? Only amateurs and burglars in a hurry did that.

Adrian's life in this secret world gradually unfolded. People usually kept what was near and dear to them close at hand in their secret hideaways, so Ian paid particular attention to everything in and around the rumpled futon bed and folding lounge chairs in the living quarters.

A dog-eared paperback copy of *The Falcon and the Snowman* on the night stand next to the bed was the first thing that caught his eye. It had Adrian's name written inside the cover. The book was about two young men who were spies, one of them a falconer who was eventually caught, some said, because of his love of the sport. Ian leafed through the pages, but found nothing of interest—no notes and no highlighted passages that would tell him something about the reader.

The book was on top of a manila folder containing a start-up kit of rules and regulations for apprentice falconers. The folder was labeled, "Government Bullshit," in felt pen. It contained notes in two different handwritings in the margins of some of the papers.

Ian began scanning the documents in the folder, still not knowing for sure what he was looking for. Adrian wasn't home and hadn't left any obvious clues to his comings and goings. The "Government Bullshit" folder was the closest thing at hand that might tell him something about Adrian—what he was up to, and where he might be at the moment. As he scanned, a pattern began to emerge, beginning with the sport of falconry. There were probably several thousand falconers in the U.S., but given the number of illegals, no one knew for sure. Most saw themselves as caretakers for the birds, and the natural environment that supported them. For many, falconry was a form of meditation that began when they flew their first bird and continued for a lifetime. Active falconers hunted with their birds at least three times a week, except when the birds were molting.

Falcons were loners that hunted on the wing and captured their prey in flight. Hawks were more sociable and hunted prey that lived on the ground. Falconers usually trained and flew both hawks and falcons, as they had for four thousand years.

When hunting with humans, the birds wore two leather straps called "jesses" attached to their legs, and small silver bells. Modern falconers also attached a small radio transmitter to the bird's tail to help find it if they became separated.

To be legal, falconers must learn state laws and how to care for the birds. They must also provide a special place for the birds called a "mews" and take a federal examination. Adrian hadn't done any of these things. The forms in the "Government Bullshit" folder were not filled out and had handwritten notes in the borders, none of them complimentary.

"The birds belong to the people" was scrawled across a printed page of government regulations. "Screw this" was written in a different, smaller handwriting across one of the other pages. The longest handwritten notation was in the smaller hand and contained a string of awkwardly worded obscenities directed against the government for "fucking with the people's falcons."

Ian finished scanning the folder and began going through the usual hiding places people think no one else has thought of. It was surprising how many there were. He didn't believe in the universal mind, but it did seem strange that so many so-called secret hiding places were used by so many people. Smuggling a handgun by taping it to the bottom of the metal base of a car jack carried in the trunk of a car was one well-known example, hiding keys and other valuables inside the base of a large table lamp was another.

Hollowed out books were perhaps the most common secret hiding places. Professionally hollowed-out books were difficult to spot, but those done by amateurs were usually uneven along the top edges where most books weren't. A quick look at the top edges of the books in the bookcase between the two lounge chairs produced an old hardcover textbook that was hollowed out. It contained a small digital camera and extra batteries.

Ian wasn't familiar with this make of digital camera, but by pressing the "MODE" button until he found the correct "Function" and "Display," he was able to review the pictures already in memory. They were of poor quality and had apparently been taken from several vantage points inside a downtown building. They looked like surveillance photos shot from behind the drapes and along the edges of windows that were low on the priority list of the window washers.

Most of the pictures were of the falcons on the ledge on the fourteenth floor of the financial center. There was also a picture of Ramsey walking out the side entrance of the building on the ground floor.

Maggie had been right. Adrian, Ramsey, the falcons and the financial center were connected. Ian didn't know the whereabouts of Adrian or Ramsey, the *who* of his inquiry, so all he had left to go on was the *where*. He would have to go to the financial center if he hoped to find out more.

Ian kept Buster close by to keep him quiet while he searched the room, but as he was putting the digital camera back in the hollowed-out book, Buster pulled away and ran to the window overlooking the alley. Ian shushed him in time to keep him from barking.

A blonde girl about Adrian's age had stopped in the alley and was getting out of an old VW van. When she saw the broken lock on the back door of the house she got back in the van, dug a cell phone out of her purse, and started to drive away. She was already talking on the phone before she was out of sight.

The police, or perhaps armed anti-government friends of the girl, were sure to show up in a few minutes. Ian snapped the leash back on Buster and tied him to the doorknob for the few minutes it took to strip two pillowcases off the bed and put the red-tailed hawk into one and the kestrel into the other. The birds were too sick to put up much of a fight. He gently placed the wrapped birds on their backs in the bottom of a paper shopping bag from a health food store, untied Buster and led him out the front door and down the street.

He and Buster had walked two blocks before a police patrol

car came by. The officers saw a man walking a dog with the leash and a plastic bag of dog poop in one hand and a shopping bag in the other. They thought nothing of it.

Chapter 10
The Nighthawk Pretext

Laura said, "Do you just want to bounce me around in bed or do you have something else in mind?"

Ian had brought Adrian's sick birds to Laura at the zoo and had walked with her to the office of the zoo veterinarian. While waiting for the vet to look at the birds he told Laura how he and Buster had found Adrian's hideaway, that Adrian wasn't there, but that he was still looking. He knew Laura would tell Maggie the address so he didn't tell her what else he had found. He didn't want Maggie to tangle with Ramsey.

Laura hadn't known about Buster, who was waiting in the car, so he told her the story of the little dog while they waited. She liked the story and said she was beginning to believe that Maggie was right, that he wasn't as bad as she had first thought he was. They both laughed at that and joked about being damned by faint praise. He had asked Laura to have dinner with him later in the week when things quieted down, which had prompted the question.

She said again, "Well, what about it? Are you just looking for casual sex or do you have something more serious in mind?"

Ian said, "Do I have a choice, or is this a test?"

"You're always so damned evasive! You've just answered my question with two of your own. Can you blame me for trying to pin you down? A woman likes to know where she stands before she gets involved in a new relationship."

Ian said, "I haven't had casual sex since the tour group of lady birders I met last year in Patagonia. The sex was great, but I had to give it up because I couldn't keep track of who was who, and who liked what."

"Now you're being a wiseass."

"How about if we just relax and have dinner together later in the week? You can give me a bad time then, while we get acquainted."

"Fair enough, but you may be sorry you asked. You don't know anything about me. I'm not who you think I am, but that doesn't mean I…"

The veterinarian returned before Laura could finish the sentence. Adrian's birds were in bad shape, but in good hands, and would eventually be returned to the wild. When they were rehabilitated and released they would be the people's birds again, although not in the narrow sense that Adrian had intended.

Laura and Ian didn't try to resume their first short, intimate conversation after the vet left and they walked back toward Laura's office. Intimate moments were like morning mists. Once gone, they were gone for good, though there may have been other mornings.

They shook hands, then held hands for a moment.

Laura said, "You're an odd bird, Ian Scott. I am too, as you'll learn when you get to know me. Call me later when you have more time. We need to talk."

As they said goodbye, Laura gave him a small calling card with only her name, Laura Cole, and a private phone number printed in silver ink. No title was given, no business affiliation revealed. Smaller and more discrete than a business card, the calling card looked as if it belonged on a silver tray in the hallway of a stately home, or in a foreign service office. He hadn't seen a card like that since he left Europe.

Buster was standing up in the driver's seat with his front paws on the steering wheel when Ian got back to his car. He took the little dog to the boarding kennel, walked him to his private quarters, and apologized for leaving him behind. Buster was staying at a first-class dog hotel, but that didn't make either one of them feel any better. The house he was house-sitting had a no-pet rule because of the allergies of the owner, so Ian had no choice.

Ian stopped by the house he was house-sitting on his way downtown to the financial center. It would be dark soon. It was time to lay the groundwork for the Nighthawk Pretext. For Ian, these techniques were second nature. He had been using birding pretexts for years, beginning with owl prowls in Europe.

The basics of a pretext were important, knowing what you're talking about, but preparing for the "what ifs" was even more important. What if a security guard or someone else checked the credentials you were using? What if the person you were expecting to meet wasn't there? What if someone didn't believe the pretext and got physical? What if, what if, what if. A competent agent covered as many of the "what ifs" as possible before going into the field. To be effective there had to be backup documentation to support the pretext, and a convincing escape and evasion plan if the pretext failed.

Ian had spent many nights watching goatsuckers, including

nightjars in Europe and nighthawks in the U.S. He had his tape recorder, binoculars, digital camera, night scope, and well-worn field guides, of course, but the Nighthawk Pretext worked best when backed up with local color. He clipped two of the zoo's brochures about native birds to one of the clipboards he used in class and added a printout from his "Wildlife Surveillance with Camera & Recorder" website.

He used one of his laptops to take a last-minute look at a local birding website, printed the home page, and circled the date at the bottom of the page in red pencil. Red penciled highlights made mundane printouts look urgent and authentic.

He then searched the website archives for articles on nighthawks and took notes based on local sources. He added his notes to the clipboard and wrote *chordeiles minor* in wide felt pen across the top of the page. The common nighthawk was less than ten inches long, but may have a wingspan of two feet. It hunted insects on the wing like a great gray swallow swooping through the night sky. It nested on bare ground and gravel rooftops, including rooftops in cities. On that night, it was the rooftops that interested Ian. He set the alarms, locked the house and drove downtown.

Ian parked his car within sight of the two security guards in the lobby of the financial center. Most of the office workers were already gone for the day and the big glass doors to the lobby were already closed. He chose the front door to present his pretext because the security guards at the front doors of office buildings dealt primarily with tenants. They were more polite and asked fewer questions than the guards at the employee's entrances or at the loading docks.

Ian got out of the car and put on a raincoat. The tape recorder and extra batteries were already in the pockets. He took his time draping himself with his camera bag and other equipment. He dropped the clipboard, then the bird book, while a sergeant and another security guard watched him from inside the lobby. By the time he reached the doors leading into the lobby, the binoculars case, camera bag and night vision scope were bouncing against his sides like saddlebags on an awkward horse. He grinned, held the clipboard up in front of him like a boarding pass with one hand, and waved the *Sibley Field Guide* around like a passport in the other. He knew he looked like a scatterbrained tourist late for a tour bus, but didn't mind. He was willing to subjugate his ego and look stupid if necessary to support the pretext.

Lip reading was an inexact science. Facial expressions were also hard to read, even when you knew the person. Ian couldn't read lips very well and didn't know the security guards, but the guard sergeant's first response to the pretext was easy to read, even through the thick plate class.

The sergeant turned toward the guard at the sign-in desk and said, "Shit, another birdbrained bird-watcher wanting to look at the falcons. I don't know what he expects to see at night. Someone will have to escort him around so he doesn't get lost in the building, or fall down a stairwell."

The guard sergeant opened the lobby door for Ian, who kept on grinning and juggling his equipment, but didn't speak. He let the sergeant jump to his own conclusions. If they supported the pretext, well and good. If not, he would know from the sergeant's reaction which of his backup techniques to use to advance the pretext, or which escape and evasion plan to use if the pretext failed completely.

The sergeant said, "Good evening, Sir. You must be part of the city bird project."

Ian nodded, "Yes indeedy. Thank you for holding the door. Do I have to sign in or something?"

The sergeant said, "Yes indeedy," in return and pointed to the sign-in book on the desk in the lobby. Ian knew he was being mocked, and that meant the pretext was probably going to work. People may be suspicious of someone who knew too much, but not of someone they thought was a fool. Ian laid the clipboard and field guide on the desk while he signed in. He looked at the other names in the log book. Ramsey's name wasn't on the list.

Both guards saw his notes on the clipboard and *Chordeiles minor* written in wide felt pen across the top of the page. Ian pointed to the scientific name for the common nighthawk and said, "Goatsuckers."

The sergeant said, "I beg your pardon?" and both he and the other guard looked startled.

Ian said, "I'm studying nighthawks. They belong to the family *caprimulgidae*, commonly referred to as goatsuckers. They nest on the roofs of buildings. I want to go up on…"

"You mean birds?"

"Yes, birds. People used to believe they suckled on goats at night. They actually eat flying insects. I was hoping that you…"

"You want to go up on the roof at night to look at birds?"

"Yes. We don't really know very much about our city goatsuckers."

The sergeant thought about that for a moment and said, "It sounds like we've got some queer birds around here."

He and the other guard laughed while Ian gathered his things together and the sergeant called for an escort. Ian knew he didn't rate one of the spit-and-polish younger guards reserved for VIPs, and certainly not a sergeant. His escort would probably be someone usually assigned to the nether regions of the building, out of the public view.

The sergeant walked him as far as the service elevators and

waited until his escort came up from the second basement. When the elevator doors opened, he introduced Ian to a sloppy overweight guard named Duane. Duane's name tag was crooked, his shirt had a coffee stain on the cuff, and his pants were much too tight. The other guards probably called him "lard ass" behind his back.

The ride to the roof on the service elevator was uneventful except for the guessing game known as, "What the hell is that smell?" Service elevators were part of the digestive tract of a building, and everything had to go somewhere. They often smelled bad and Duane added another layer of unidentified scent to the mix.

When they reached the top floor, Duane got off the elevator first and led the way up the long ramp leading to the roof. Ian stopped him before he opened the security door.

Ian said, "Thank you so much for your help. I appreciate it. I know you have more important things to do than escort me around the building. Would you be insulted if I offered to pay you a little extra for your time?"

Duane had seemed bored on the way up on the elevator, but perked up at the mention of money. He said, "A little extra is always good."

The guard's use of the word, "always," triggered Ian's next question. He asked, "What do the other people pay you? I want to be fair."

"I've been helping a P.I. He usually slips me a twenty or so."

"That sounds fair."

Ian gave Duane a twenty-dollar bill from a money clip in his pocket, not out of his wallet. Why expose what you have in your wallet, even a pretext wallet? Duane's mention of a P.I. triggered the next question while Ian still had his money clip in his hand.

He said, "I don't know what you do for the private eye, so I don't know if a twenty is enough."

"I unlock doors and stuff like that. He has to go out on the roof to set up the staging for the ornithologists for the next day, run wires for those guys, and other things. It takes a long time, but he has a building pass so I don't have to hang around like I do with other people."

"Have you seen the private eye tonight?"

"No."

"Does he have to sign in?"

"Yea, sure."

"Do you loan him your keys?"

"Sometimes. Ramsey's a licensed P.I., you know, so that's okay. I wouldn't loan the keys to just anybody, so don't even ask."

This was the first time Duane had used Ramsey's name. The pieces of the puzzle were coming together. Ian didn't react to the name and continued the pretext.

"I understand completely. I won't ask you to loan me your keys, but I would appreciate it if you'd stand by here while I go out on the roof and look for nighthawks. If we open the door the light from in here will scare them away."

"What do you want me to do?"

"Can we turn off these inside lights long enough for me to go out the door to the roof? You can turn the lights back on as soon as you close the door behind me."

"How you gonna see what you're doing?"

"I've got a night scope and a flashlight with an infrared filter. You can't see the light from the flashlight, but I can see the birds when I look through my night scope. I just need you to stand by here while I look around outside."

Duane said, "What if I get a security call on the radio while you're out on the roof? I might have to go and check on something."

"No problem. When I'm done, I'll come back inside, and if you're not here, I'll wait until you get back. I'll need you to escort me back down to the lobby, and that's worth another twenty. I can pay you now, if you like."

Duane liked, and the money changed hands. He told Ian that if he had to leave on a call, he wouldn't be gone for more than an hour. Ian guessed that the guard just wanted some unscheduled time to himself. He promised to wait. Duane turned off the inside lights and opened the door out onto the roof for Ian.

Ian waited until the guard closed the door behind him, then stepped to one side and switched on the night scope. Some light filtered up from the streets far below and across from the other buildings, but the center of the roof was in deep shadows. Ian scanned slowly from side to side. The roof seemed deserted.

He dropped to one knee, switched on the flashlight with the infrared filter, and shone it across the roof at roof level. If you dropped a contact lens on the floor and shone an ordinary flashlight across the floor at floor level, the lens may be highlighted. If you shone a flashlight along a wall where you thought a hole may have been drilled from the other side to plant a small eavesdropping device, the hole may be highlighted. Ian was using the same technique with infrared light and a night scope. He hoped to find and photograph a nesting nighthawk on the flat gravel roof, or perhaps some eggs. If not, he would at least go through the motions to cover himself and support the pretext.

He didn't find any nests, but took several pictures of flying nighthawks silhouetted against the night sky. Taken from the kneeling position, the birds looked larger and closer than they really were because there were no reference points in the photos. He also recorded some of the sounds the birds made as they swooped nearby. The pictures and recordings supported the pretext.

Ian stood up and began walking. Switching back and forth between the camera, night scope and binoculars gave him an excuse to walk the entire roof and look at the surrounding buildings.

He paid particular attention to the new railings around the edge of the roof. They were made of galvanized pipe and were installed as part of the upgrade of the building infrastructure during the recent remodel. He was looking for signs of digiscoping and found them on the railing on the north side of the building.

Ramsey had mentioned digiscoping several times in birding class, but the private eye was acting like a spy, not a birder. Birders take long-range photos by putting a digital camera up against the eyepiece of a spotting scope to obtain a level of magnification that far exceeds that of a conventional camera lens. Digital images could also be enhanced through the use of software, a plus for birders and for spies.

There were problems. For digiscoping to achieve the fantastic results it did the camera, the spotting scope, and the mount would have to be as stable as possible while pictures were being taken. A spy would have to either carry a clumsy tripod, which was difficult to conceal, or use strong metal clamps to fasten the digiscope setup to something solid.

There were clamp marks halfway along the railing on the north side of the roof. Sculptors found tiny imperfections in the stone they were working by magnifying the delicate touch in their fingertips with a thin piece of cloth. Ian found the serrated teeth marks of the digiscope clamps by sliding a handkerchief along the railing.

There was no way to tell for sure where the digiscope had been pointed. Ian could only brace his elbows on the railing above the clamp marks and scan the surrounding buildings. His binoculars were now of more use than the night scope.

There were several lit windows in the building directly across from him, easy targets for espionage, including espionage by exposure. This simple form of spying required only that an accomplice, willing or otherwise, leave business secrets or other valuable information exposed where it could be copied by digiscoping.

Photos, blueprints and drawings were intentionally left exposed near a window to be copied. Secrets were purposely left unattended on computer screens, or read over someone's shoulder. E-mails, faxes and other forms of written communications were exposed, and photographed. The financial district in any city was home to many secrets.

So, was Ramsey a spy-for-hire, a voyeur, or both? Was there a difference? Ian had spent many nights on surveillance, and often felt like a voyeur himself. What he saw might have nothing to do with his assignment, but he wouldn't know that until later, when all the reports were in. Some of the things he had seen over the years had been totally unexpected.

Ian scanned the buildings directly across from him, but saw nothing of interest. He looked farther afield. As he scanned down the side streets away from the financial district the neighborhood changed as it often does in big cities. An elegant old hotel caught his eye. Ian knew something of the hotel's history, but not of its present use.

The small hotel had once been a playground for after-work playmates from the financial district, illicit lovers taking a sex break before they went home to the suburbs. Those days were past, though the stories lingered.

The hotel was now a private club and no longer open to the public. The hotel signs were gone and the main entrance seldom used except for special functions. At this time of night the lobby was closed and the drapes were drawn. Members who used the club after hours came and went anonymously through the key controlled parking garage in the basement.

Ian was about to continue scanning the rest of the neighborhood when the lights went on in one of the rooms near the top floor of the private club. He was looking directly down into the room as a woman entered, followed by a waiter pushing a room-service trolley. The woman was tall and distinguished-looking, wore an expensive grey silk suit, and had long blonde hair.

The woman was Muriel Blair! The same Muriel who had run over his foot with her car years before, when they had served together at the consulate in Frankfurt. Their paths had crossed from time to time since then, but he hadn't spoken to her since returning to the U.S. She was still a beautiful woman, and was obviously aging far better than he was.

He knew that Muriel had left the foreign service and was now active in politics at the national level. He had seen her on television, and in the local papers. He knew she was in town with some of the people from the planning committee of her party, but had no idea why she was at the private club at this time of night.

Muriel tipped the waiter rather than signing a chit, which probably meant she was a guest, not a regular member. When the waiter left, she began taking off her clothes. When she was down to her designer underwear, she put on a silk dressing gown from an overnight bag and began unpacking the rest of the luggage that was stowed on the lower shelf of the room service cart.

What was she doing at a small private club near the financial district? Why all the luggage? She was a house guest at a magnificent home on the lake on this visit, according to the papers, and had stayed at the usual upscale hotels on previous trips.

Muriel took a folder of eight-by-ten photos from the suitcase, spread them out on the dresser, and started unpacking the rest of the luggage. She began redecorating the room by replacing the hotel bedspread with one she brought with her. Nothing in the room escaped her attention. She replaced everything removable with something of her own, including the faded picture on the wall above the bed.

Muriel looked at the photos several times as she worked, but Ian couldn't see what was in the pictures until she took them from the dresser and spread them out on the bed. The photos were of the room as it had looked when the club had been a hotel, several years in the past. As Ian scanned the room he could see that the furnishings she had brought with her were duplicates of the ones in the old photos. The only new items were her CD player and an album of customized disks. She had turned the clock back, and was setting the stage for something.

Muriel removed the cover on the top shelf of the room-service trolley left behind by the waiter. The cart held trays of hors d'oeuvres, a single red rose in a small crystal vase, a bowl of ice, and an empty ice bucket.

Muriel took a bottle of sparkling rose from one of the suitcases, placed it in the ice bucket on a slant so that the label showed, and poured ice around it. The wine was now out of fashion, but had been popular back when the hotel had been a playground for illicit lovers.

Muriel looked at the old photos spread out on the bed one

124

more time, then put them away in the folder. She stood back with her hands on her hips to admire the setting, then smiled to herself and moved the rose in the crystal vase from the service cart to the bedside table.

She was standing there looking around the room, apparently lost in thought, when she suddenly turned toward the door. She said something, then struck a provocative pose as the door to the room swung open.

A heavy-set gray-haired man with a puzzled look on his face came into the room, glanced around, and closed the door behind him. He came forward to kiss Muriel, then stopped and looked more closely at his surroundings. His puzzled look changed to one of astonishment, as if he had just stepped back in time. He took it all in, then tried to say something, but stopped abruptly as if overwhelmed by nostalgia.

Muriel kissed him, then pointed to the wine chilling in the wine bucket. The man was still looking around the room as he started to open the bottle, then stopped and stared at the label as if he couldn't believe what he saw. The wine meant something to him, as it did to her. She laughed, and the past swept over them both like the sounds of old songs on new CDs. His hand shook as he poured the wine and she dimmed the lights. They talked, drank wine, nibbled at the hors d'oeuvres, and kissed again.

They both laughed as Muriel took another bottle of the old-fashioned sparkling rose from her luggage. The first bottle had provided a link to their past, the new bottle looked to the future.

Muriel and the man were obviously lovers. She was still having secret affairs on her own terms in prearranged settings as she had with him in Frankfurt, but now her affairs were apparently lasting longer. Her affairs had matured. His had not.

Ian envied her, and wished her luck. He still found it difficult to establish long term relationships, especially with the strong-willed women he found the most attractive.

Were Muriel and the heavy-set man in the room with her targets? There were dozens of possible espionage target locations within range of Ian's binoculars, many more within range of a digiscope. Was this what it seemed, lovers reliving old times, or were there other, less obvious meanings and motives? Espionage, perhaps, or blackmail, or both? In Ian's world, when substitute furnishings were put in place in a room—any room—it was usually because the new items had built-in bugs.

Ian had been focused on Muriel—how she was dressed and what she was doing. The scene began to make more sense when he took a closer look at the man who was with her. The man was a mover and shaker in the opposing political party. He and Muriel were supposed to be bitter rivals! They were always at each other's throats in public, high profile confrontations on talk shows and elsewhere that helped them both promote their political careers. If the media became aware of their secret romantic ties the political pundits would cut them to ribbons. Ian could visualize the headlines. It would start with "Sleeping with the Enemy" in the main stream press, but soon degenerate to "Screwing the Voters," and worse, in the tabloids. The public would feel they'd been tricked and exploited. Muriel's political career would be ruined.

The videotape of Muriel and the man in the room could be used to blackmail them both. The scene suggested other secret meetings between the two, going back a number of years. Were the lovers both targets? They both had access to inside information that would be valuable to those involved with political and economic espionage. Ian would probably never know if they were targets unless their affair became public knowledge. They had nothing to fear from him, in any case.

Ian wondered if he were the man in the hotel room, would his own suspicions of espionage have poisoned the evening? What tender moments had he missed in his own personal life because of his profession?

The intimate scene unfolding before him raised other questions as well, ones that had nagged him throughout his career. Was it possible to perform a surveillance without violating the privacy of innocent people, even if only by accident? He thought not. Who knew what was going to happen, before it happened? Who had twenty-twenty foresight? The questions continued but didn't stop him from doing stakeouts and other types of surveillance.

Ian lowered his binoculars as Muriel and the man began to caress each other as a prelude to sex. Enough was enough. This wasn't getting him anywhere in his own investigation. He hadn't seen anything from the roof of the financial center that tied Ramsey to Adrian's disappearance, or that proved that Ramsey was a spy. He moved away from his observation post on the roof and went farther along the rail.

Ian took a close look at the window washer's staging that was parked on the roof. The mechanism that raised and lowered the staging over the side of the building was locked off. The padlock could easily be shimmed open, but he didn't have time to use the staging and it didn't fit the nighthawk pretext.

He looked over the side, but didn't expect any breakthroughs. If Ramsey was using the staging to prowl around the outside of the building on foggy nights, as Ian suspected, the P.I. wouldn't leave anything behind that could be tied directly to him. It is almost impossible to identify the owner of a tiny audio/video bug, even if someone is lucky enough to find it. Ramsey would be using the latest, which usually means the smallest eavesdropping devices.

Ian couldn't see the falcon's nest either. The birds were down on the fourteenth floor, below the overhang. He had no logical reason to go down there, and again, it wasn't part of the pretext.

The nighthawk pretext itself was working well, but producing nothing. His mentor had sung a silly song over drinks after graduation, some final words of advice to a new trainee before sending him out in the field. Something about patience and fortitude, patience and fortitude, and things would go your way. Well, his patience and fortitude were running out, and so were his options.

Ian opened the security door on the roof and went down the ramp to the top floor of the building. The nightlights were on in the hallway, but Duane wasn't there. He had been out on the roof for more than an hour and had expected to find the guard waiting. Pretexts often provided unexpected openings and Ian was quick to take advantage of this one.

Since Duane wasn't there to escort him down to the lobby, Ian had a good excuse to go looking for him, an excuse to prowl the building. The guard couldn't say much, since he wasn't supposed to leave him alone in the first place.

Ian walked down the hallway and looked around the corner. He couldn't see very far down the corridor, the nightlights being not very bright, but by putting his head next to the wall he could hear someone speaking softly as the sound traveled along the hard surface. Pilgrims who climbed the stairs to the dome of Saint Peter's in Rome could put their ears to the wall and hear the soft murmur of prayers being said on the far side of the dome. Ian was using the same technique along the wall in the financial center, but was hearing what sounded like garbled curses, not prayers. He moved quietly in that direction.

Duane was ahead of him in the hallway, trying to get his passkey to work on the side door to one of the office suites. Each of the suites on that floor had a main entrance used by the office staff and the clients, and a private entrance reserved for the executive in charge. The executive's entrance opened into a private dressing room, one of the perks expected by managers at that level.

The door to the private entrance was stuck and Duane was cursing it under his breath. He bumped it with a fat hip and it finally opened. Ian saw a woman's suit in a dry-cleaner's bag hanging next to an armoire as the security guard went inside the dressing room and locked the door behind him. Duane was a long way from the second basement, the nether region from which he'd been summoned for escort duty, and was probably up to no good.

Ian considered his options. He wanted to stay within the boundaries of the pretext. To do otherwise was to invite disaster, but this new development was another unexpected opening, one too good to pass up. It might provide the breakthrough he needed.

Ian moved up to the dressing-room door, listened for a minute, then took the small tape recorder from his raincoat pocket. The recorder was German-made, had several stages of amplification, and worked well with a number of different microphones. He unplugged the microphone he had used to record bird sounds on the roof and plugged in a contact mic.

When he held the contact microphone to the dressing-room door and turned up the volume to the earphone he could hear Duane breathing on the other side of the door! Duane had his ear to the door and was listening for sounds in the hallway.

Ian stood still and waited. If he walked away, Duane might hear him go. If he stayed where he was there would be a confrontation if Duane opened the door. His pretext would probably be blown, in either case.

Duane kept his ear to the door for another minute. When he thought the coast was clear, Ian heard him move away from the door and open the armoire.

He heard coat hangers slide along the bar in the armoire as Duane rummaged through the woman's clothes. He stopped and sniffed at something at that height, something on one of the hangers.

Ian heard what was happening next as a series of zippers. First the sound of a heavy zipper being opened near the floor, a shoe bag perhaps, then Duane opening another zipper at waistline height. While he was trying to guess what was going on in the dressing room he heard several short grunts in quick succession, sounds that created an unpleasant mental image of what was happening on the other side of the door. They also provided another opening that was too good to pass up.

Ian tapped on the dressing-room door.

"Duane, is that you? Are you all right?"

Ian heard zippers again, first the one at waist height, then the one on the shoe bag.

"Duane, are you okay? Should I call the guard sergeant?"

Ian barely had time to put the microphone, ear piece and recorder back in his raincoat pocket before Duane opened the door.

"Don't call the sergeant! I'm okay, I was just looking around."

"You were making strange noises. What were you doing in there?"

"I was just looking around."

Ian stepped into the doorway before Duane could close the door.

"Are you supposed to be checking the dressing rooms?"

Duane's face showed that he didn't like the questions and was frightened by what might happen next.

"I go all over the building. That's my job. Don't call the sergeant, okay?"

"If you say so. I guess it's all right, since you've got your own passkeys. The sergeant must trust you."

"Sarge knows I go all over the building."

Ian knew Duane was lying. He also knew Duane would now be anxious to change the subject and might talk, and keep on talking, if Ian talked about something else and primed the conversational pump.

Ian said, "That must be nice for Ramsey, the private eye you're helping."

"What do you mean?"

"You having your own passkeys, and the run of the building."

"Oh, yea, that."

Ian said, "I know Ramsey works for the attorney who sponsors the city bird project. What else does he do? He can't make a living doing volunteer work."

"Why are you asking about Ramsey?"

"I've always been curious about private eyes. You said you sometimes loaned him your passkeys. You must know something about him."

"Well, I might know something. Do we have to talk here in the doorway?"

Ian said, "We can talk by the elevator, before we go down to the lobby. Private eyes are fascinating! I'd appreciate whatever you can tell me."

Duane heard the implied threat: "Talk! If I like what I hear, I won't tell the sergeant that you went off by yourself to prowl that woman's dressing room."

Duane closed the dressing room door and locked it behind him. He was quiet as they walked to the elevator. Ian knew he was trying to decide if he really had to talk to this silly birder. How much could the birdbrain know? Anyway, wasn't it the birder's word against his?

Getting people to talk was often a step-by-step process. The number of steps required depended on a number of factors, including the strength of character of the subject. Duane caved in immediately when Ian took the contact microphone and tape recorder from his raincoat pocket, popped out the tape, and dropped it into an inside pocket of his jacket.

Duane said, "So what do you want to know?"

Ian asked questions, and used the answers to keep the conversation going. Once started, Duane told everything he knew about Ramsey, bits and pieces forced out by the desire to focus attention away from himself.

Ian asked where Ramsey lived. Duane said the private eye owned a castle. According to Duane, Ramsey's exact words were, "A man's home is his castle, and I have a castle on wheels."

Ian asked where Ramsey went when he borrowed the master keys. Duane said Ramsey went off alone, so he wasn't sure. He did know that Ramsey liked to visit "the fancy places," the boardrooms, office suites, executive health club areas, and the ornate women's washroom on the fourteenth floor. The one they wrote about in the newspaper.

Ian said, "Are you sure about the washroom on the fourteenth floor?"

"Yea. I seen him come out of there more than once. Ramsey is some kind of weirdo, hanging out in the women's toilet. He's got no reason to be in there. Not like me. I got to make my rounds, and check things out."

Ian nodded, but thought, you want me to believe that Ramsey is a worse pervert than you are. That's not much of a defense.

Ian asked Duane if Ramsey used a cell phone. He said yes, but the one conversation he overheard didn't make any sense. It was mostly about numbers. Ian knew that meant Ramsey used numbered "contract codes" when talking with his employer. He used them himself. These simple codes were based on random numbers assigned to the important people, places and things on the original contract or work assignment. In use, the numbers sounded like engineering jargon.

Ian asked the security guard if he ever saw Ramsey use a pay phone. Duane said he saw Ramsey use the "fuck phone" twice, the pay phone in the alcove next to the alley exit. Ian knew Duane meant the telephone investigators call the "fools' phone," the closest anonymous outside line. Ramsey wouldn't be fool enough to make his own calls from there, so he must have the pay phone bugged.

There was more. Duane provided bits and pieces of information, much of which didn't make sense at the moment but might be important later. When he had squeezed all the odds and ends he was likely to get out of Duane, Ian reached past him and pushed the "down" button on the elevator. This simple act made it clear who was now in charge. Duane was quiet on the way down in the elevator, but seemed relieved when Ian went back to talking about birds.

The follow-up portion of a pretext was very important. Done well, it prevented awkward questions during the last phase of the pretext performance and reduced the likelihood of exposure later when people have second thoughts.

Ian used the nighthawk pictures and recordings he had

made while out on the roof to full advantage with the security guards in the lobby. As he signed out he looked at the other names in the logbook, as he had when he signed in. Ramsey's name still wasn't on the list.

Ian talked birding until the guards were so bored they could hardly wait to get him out of the building. As the saying went, "First bore them with facts, then blind them with bullshit."

Ian asked the guard sergeant if Duane could escort him out the side door. He said he wanted to shoot some more pictures of nighthawks against the night sky without being flooded by light from the front of the building. The alley would be dark and the outline of the building would provide a dramatic backdrop. He started to explain the digital camera settings, but no one was interested.

The guard at the sign-out desk mumbled something that sounded like "artsy fartsy" under his breath, but Ian pretended not to notice. The sergeant was glad to see Ian go, and more than happy to have Duane continue as escort. He said, "Good luck with those goatsuckers!" and sent them on their way.

Duane had been sweating it out as Ian wound down the Nighthawk Pretext. His relief at not being exposed now made him willing to do whatever Ian asked.

When they were out of sight of the lobby, Ian said he needed to go to the bathroom and would let himself out the alley door when he was ready. He told Duane to go back downstairs and go on about his business.

He watched as Duane went down the back stairwell, two turns down to the second basement. Duane looked up as he opened the basement door. Ian waved.

Duane didn't wave back.

Chapter 11
The Fools' Phone

Duane, the fat security guard, had said he saw Ramsey use the pay phone in the alcove next to the alley exit. Duane called it the "fuck phone." Investigators called it the "fools' phone," the closest anonymous outside line that people in office buildings use to call prostitutes, order illegal drugs, and make other foolish moves that endanger their lives and their livelihoods.

The captains of industry didn't use the fools' phone, but their staff members did. Those low and mid-level staffers had fewer financial incentives, were less loyal, and were more willing to sell out the company to save themselves from the threats of a blackmailer. The fools' phone was a blackmail-rich environment for eavesdroppers.

Ian knew that Ramsey wouldn't make his own calls from the fools' phone, so there had to be another reason for his comings and goings. He must of had the phone booth bugged. What Duane had seen was probably Ramsey picking up recordings from a self-contained bug in the booth. A recorder would be the eavesdropper's tool of choice since transmitting bugs didn't work very well inside office buildings, which were already full of other electronics.

Ian was alone in the darkened hallway near the alley exit. The bug in the booth would probably be voice-activated, but spies were not restricted to audio eavesdropping. Audio/video devices as small as a tube of lipstick were common. A bug in the fools's phone would probably include a miniature camera.

Why would a spy record only the audio portion of a conversation between a manager and an escort service as the man described in detail the sex acts he had in mind? A pinhole camera would capture and record the entire sweaty-faced conversation. The pictures would also make surveillance easier when it was time to follow the target and tighten the noose.

Why would a spy record only an accountant's voice as she arranged to meet her drug supplier? An audio/video bug with a pinhole camera would capture a close-up of her face. The video could then be enhanced to help the spy see past her dark glasses or other amateur disguises.

Telephone booths in office buildings had come and gone, and come back again, primarily because the public got tired of open phones and shoulder surfers. The phone booth in the alcove near the alley exit was one of the new ones made to look old, a concept beloved of young designers. It was painted red and had a sign that read, "Telefon," over the doorway.

Ian approached the phone booth with caution. The door was open. He knew that a voice-activated video recorder would probably be the eavesdropper's tool of choice for this location, but there was always something new on the spy-tech market. New equipment. New attacks. Some eavesdroppers even tapped into a building's 110-volt electrical system to hot-wire the bug and discourage debuggers. One more thing to worry about as he wound down the Nighthawk Pretext.

Most birders carried a hat with them when they got into the field. Often a rolled-up Irish tweed walking hat, a broad-brimmed canvas tuckaway, or an old felt floppy shoved down in the bottom of a camera bag. Ian wore one hat and carried a second to wear when he wanted to look different. Changing hats changed the outline of a person's face and head, if nothing else. It wouldn't hide his identity if he was looking directly at a hidden camera at head height in a phone booth, but it would hide his face in the dimly lit booth below eye level.

Ian left the phone booth door open so that the light stayed off, tilted his birding hat forward, and began his search of the booth at waist level. Experience is a great teacher. He knew approximately what to look for, where to look, and how to identify the device when he found it.

A small voice-activated video recorder was fastened up under the shelf in the back of the booth and was painted to look like telephone company equipment. A pinhole camera and the wire connecting it to the recorder were built into the molding at head height. It was a professional job, one probably done by substitution.

Ramsey would have photographed the piece of original molding, made a copy of it in his workshop, and installed the camera and wiring inside. To plant the bug he would pop off the original molding and substitute his own, the work of a few minutes. Installing the recorder where he could easily change the tapes would take only a few minutes longer. Then it was just a matter of visiting the phone booth from time to time, leaning on the shelf while making a call to mask what he was doing, and switching the videotapes.

Ian stole the videotape from the recorder, tucked it in with his own equipment, and let himself out the alley exit.

He took three more photos from the alley, framing the surrounding buildings against the night sky. A nighthawk passed high overhead as it dove toward the freeway park, but he missed the camera shot.

He was walking down the alley toward his car when Ramsey jumped down from the loading dock at the other end of the building and cut across the street to the parking garage. He was carrying a black nylon garment bag over his shoulder and walking so fast he was almost running.

Ramsey drove out of the parking garage a few minutes later. He was driving an older sedan Ian hadn't seen before and was heading off down the street in the other direction.

Chapter 12
Old Crows &
Cleaning Stations

A rolling surveillance had to be carefully planned in advance, especially one run at night. Team members, vehicles and surveillance equipment had to be selected and moved into position. Surveillance teams consisting of at least three vehicles, with a driver and leg man in each, had the best chance of success. The leg man kept the other teams informed by radio as the surveillance progressed and left the vehicle to proceed on foot, if necessary.

Ian had none of these resources available when he left the financial center to follow Ramsey. He was on his own. Ramsey had already merged with the nighttime traffic before Ian got to his car and pulled away from the curb.

He hung back, watched the taillights up ahead, and waited. The downtown traffic was light at this time of night, but steady. It included the usual mix of taxis, delivery trucks and private vehicles driven by people out looking for entertainment.

The first few minutes of a rolling surveillance were crucial. The initial contact would likely be made where the target parked his vehicle and continue on from there. A rolling surveillance began with what rolled; how smart did the target have to be to know that? A suspicious person watched his rearview mirrors when he first pulled away from a parking place, even when running routine errands. Ramsey had been in the financial center without signing in or out at the security desk in the lobby, and had left in a hurry through an unauthorized exit. He was sure to be watching his back.

Had Ramsey had time to check the fools' phone booth and find that the videotape was missing? Or had he been servicing eavesdropping devices somewhere else, in or around the building? If so, had he seen Ian?

What was Ramsey carrying in the nylon garment bag, the spy's ubiquitous all-purpose carrier of choice in an urban setting? Had he removed the recorder from the fools' phone booth or other eavesdropping equipment elsewhere in the financial center? Was he shutting down the operation and in the process of covering his tracks?

Ian still had more questions than answers, and the questions kept coming. He knew that following Ramsey by himself was pushing his luck, but this new development was another unexpected opening that was too good to pass up.

A white delivery truck pulled into traffic behind Ramsey, one of the high-box walk-in vans that were the workhorses of city commerce. It partially blocked Ramsey's view to the rear and allowed Ian to work his way up in traffic. He stayed two cars back behind the van, out of Ramsey's line of sight, but at risk of losing contact.

If he followed Ramsey too closely and was spotted, Ramsey

would take evasive action—do something crazy, perhaps—or at least wouldn't go where he had originally intended. If he stayed too far back, he might lose contact with Ramsey. Ian moved up one car in the line of traffic and hoped that he wasn't too close.

Ramsey worked his way north, out of the downtown traffic, and onto Queen Anne Hill. When he left the main drag and began to cut through the neighborhood at the top of the hill, Ian began to worry. The homes and apartment buildings were set close to the street, some almost overhanging the sidewalk. It was an ideal place for a cleaning station.

Crows visited anthills and used the ants to clean their feathers of fleas and other parasites. Some old crows have favorite anthills, and returned to them again and again. Cleaning stations were common in nature, even among fishes.

Spooks and spies and private eyes used the services of human cleaners. They drove by a prearranged location where the cleaner could easily see if they were being followed, video the follower, and call ahead to alert the person being followed. This service was sometimes performed by a friend or a family member in the private sector, but more often by a professional cleaner with high-tech counter-surveillance equipment.

Ian spotted the cleaner in the bay window on the first floor of one of the houses on the left, near the middle of the block. It was only a fleeting impression, a face behind a lace curtain partly lit by a streetlight, but he knew the face. He also knew there would be a security camera behind the curtain, and at least two other cameras under the building's overhang covering the street in both directions.

There was now no point in continuing the surveillance. The cleaner would probably call Ramsey on a cell phone to tell him that he was being followed and Ramsey would be waiting to turn the tables a few blocks ahead. The rolling surveillance would then become a game of cat and mouse or perhaps a high-speed chase, either one of which would be unproductive, especially at that time of night. In any case, Ramsey wouldn't give anything away if he knew he was being followed.

Ian stopped, turned around in the middle of the street as if he were lost, and went back the way he had come. He made a right turn at the next corner and parked in the shadows, out of sight of the bay window.

A privet hedge and two backyard fences later, he was at the back door of the house looking through the glass panel. He had landed awkwardly on his weak ankle going over the last fence, but that was the least of his problems. A motion detector turned on the lights in the back yard and framed him in the doorway.

Lewis Hayes was standing in the hallway, leaning on a walker, and pointing a short-barreled shotgun in his direction. A dog, a big ugly Rottweiler mix, was standing stiff-legged on alert beside him, waiting for the word to attack.

When Lewis saw who it was, he grinned, put the shotgun crossways on the basket of the walker, and shuffled his way down the hall toward the back door. The dog was still on alert, but eased off on command, and sat down when he was told.

Lewis said, "What the hell are you doing here?"

"I was following your client."

"Yes, I know. I was about to call him when I saw it was you who had him under surveillance. Are you by yourself?"

"Yes."

"Then I take it this isn't official business."

"No, but I think it soon will be. This guy—I know him as Ramsey—is a private eye working as a spy."

"He told me some crazy ladies were following him around, a

domestic matter. It sounded like legitimate work."

Ian said, "One woman he had a run-in with is dead. I think he killed her. Another woman has a missing grandson and is trying to track him down. Ramsey may also have killed the grandson."

"Son of a bitch! Let me call this guy off, then tell me the rest of the story."

Lewis let Ian in, locked the door behind them, and reset the alarms. He left the dog to watch the door. He began the slow shuffle back to the front of the house, then had second thoughts, sat down on the seat of the walker and got on the cell phone.

Lewis's conversation with Ramsey was short but convincing. He told Ramsey that whoever was following him was lost and cruising the neighborhood. He'd seen a car going back and forth on the cross streets, but not close enough for the cameras. He made it sound as if Ramsey had lost his pursuer on his own, good work by a good driver. People liked to believe the best about themselves and their skills, so it made a good story. Lewis let it go at that. He told Ramsey there wouldn't be a cleaning charge since there weren't any pictures, said he was sorry he couldn't be of service, and hung up the phone.

Lewis said, "That's the last time I clean for him. We better go watch the monitors in case he doubles back."

He led the way to the front of the house—a slow process, and one that was obviously painful. He switched from the walker to a barber's chair bolted to the floor next to the bay window and waved Ian into a straight-backed chair against the inside wall.

The streetlight outside barely lit the room. The rest of the light, what little there was, came from the surveillance equipment. Lewis was working in an urban setting where there was usually at least some light available, even at night, so most of his gear was for light enhancement and not for seeing in total darkness.

The video monitors sat on brackets below the window sills, tilted for easy viewing. Lewis swivelled the barber's chair around so that he could watch the monitors while talking with Ian. He tried to ease the pain of his back and legs by adjusting the chair, but was only partially successful. He had learned to live with the pain, but had never learned to accept it. He was a former soldier—a fighter, not an acceptor.

Lewis said, "So what's your part in this, official or unofficial?"

"At this point I'm not sure. I began by helping the grandmother look for the missing grandson. Now the agency is also interested, but I'm not sure why."

"That sounds about right. They don't tell you much once you're out of the loop. You must be on somebody's shit list or you wouldn't be working alone."

"They keep in touch. I teach a few classes and run a few errands."

"Classes at the DIA?"

"No. I teach wildlife surveillance classes for birders at the local zoo. Some of the students call it Spy School."

"Teaching bird-watchers? Man, you've either come way down in the world or have the world's best cover story."

Ian said, "Terrorists take flying lessons. Spies of all kinds take spying lessons. Many of the worst threats to our world begin in a class somewhere."

"Can you make a living teaching?"

"It's the best I can do at the moment. What about you? The last I heard you were in the VA hospital."

"Ain't it a bitch? Life is hard, and then you die. We started out to save the world, I end up a crippled old soldier running a cleaning station, and you end up teaching bird-watchers in the park."

Lewis had been watching the video monitors as they talked, letting his eyes flick from one to the other, seldom moving his head. This forced eye movement counteracts the tendency to stare, a common problem for those who watch monitors for long periods of time at a fixed distance. Ian was also watching the monitors. He saw an older sedan that looked like the one Ramsey had been driving, but Lewis shook his head before he could ask the question.

Lewis said, "Same make, different model. This one belongs to a nurse that lives in the duplex at the end of the block. She works nights."

The dog at the back door was getting restless. They could hear his nails scrape the floor in the hallway as he shifted position. He didn't know what was going on, but heard them talking, and didn't want to be left out.

Lewis said, "Felonious worries when I'm out of his sight for more than a few minutes, especially when there is someone else in the house. We're alone most of the time. I'd better call him in. Don't make any sudden moves until he sees that you're not a threat."

Lewis spoke to the dog in German. The dog trotted down the hall and into the front room, head up and ready for trouble. Lewis had him sit between them. Ian sat still and let the dog look him over.

"Felonious?"

"His full name is Felonious Assault. I got him as a pup from the dog pound, something I learned from you. He's ugly as sin, but smart as a whip."

"An odd name."

"I introduce him by name when strangers come to the door. Anyone casing the place is put on notice. The name alone is a great deterrent."

"I take it you're not worried about home invaders."

"I'd let Felonious speak for himself in that situation."

The dog took notice each time he heard his name, his big head swinging back and forth. Lewis said something in German which helped him relax, though he still kept his eyes on Ian.

Lewis said, "You had a dog with you when you came to see me in the hospital. They had just started letting dogs visit and I always looked forward to that. We all did. I moved on to the rehab center and lost track. That was a long time ago, so I don't suppose you still have the mutt."

"I moved on too to another assignment. I couldn't take the dog, but found him a home before I left, a good home with a family with kids. I've got another dog-pound dog now, a smart little terrier mix named Buster."

Lewis said, "Death row dogs are always the smartest, even if they aren't the best-looking. The dogs in the cages at the back of the dog pound, waiting to be put down. Crossbreeds who were cute pups, but are now too ugly for adoption. Old gray dogs abandoned by owners who don't want to pay the vet bills. Disposable critters. It don't seem right, but I guess in the end we are all disposable critters, including you and me."

They were both still watching the video monitors as they talked. They might have been two old friends watching a ball game on cable TV except that they never completely relaxed, or took their eyes off the screens.

Ian said, "I heard you were decorated for pulling some troopers from the wreck when your chopper went down. That's a good way to get a medal."

Lewis said, "The best way to get a medal is standing on your own two feet on the parade ground somewhere. Mine was pinned to my hospital gown, but at least I'm alive. We both know the worst way to get a medal. The ones who get those are the real heroes."

"I met someone who was there. You deserved the decoration."

"If you don't mind, I'd rather talk about something else."

Ian nodded, watched the video monitors, and waited for Lewis to begin a new topic. Lewis swivelled the outside cameras back and forth to cover the street in front of the building and part of the intersections at the ends of the block. He began speaking again while still manipulating the remote controls.

"Does anyone still use the cleaning station beginning at the Irish café in the alley above the Pike Place Market?"

"I don't know."

"I used to sit in the oyster bar at the foot of the wooden stairs that led down to the market, or at one of the outside tables. Anyone following the person I was cleaning for was on stage as they came down the stairs from the alley. It was perfect for pictures. Everyone takes pictures at the market, even the locals, so I didn't stand out. Man, those were the days."

"Ramsey apparently uses the market from time to time, I'm not sure for what."

"Oh, yea? I'm not surprised. You can enter the market a dozen ways, and leave by a dozen others. It's a perfect place to shake off a tail, or meet people, including visitors from all over."

"Do you have any idea what Ramsey is doing, other than using your services?"

"Not a clue. This is the first time he's used the service. We talked on the phone and agreed on a price, like I always do. Then he called tonight to tell me he would be coming by. I'm here most of the time, so I can take cleaning jobs on short notice, and charge accordingly."

"How did he learn about your service?"

"I don't know. Most of my clients are government types, past or present. I don't advertise, so it must have been by word-of-mouth. They call, I clean. They pay in cash, usually by courier. That's about it. They like it like that, and so do I."

Ian said, "That's the way it is with most of the people who take my classes. I don't know much about them, and don't need to. It's different with Ramsey, but I haven't had much luck tracking him down. None of the usual Internet searches have turned up anything. Even the address on his private investigator's license is a dead end. He must have a safe house, and probably a workshop, but I don't know where."

"He sounds slippery. Sorry I can't be more help."

They watched the monitors for another half hour. There wasn't much traffic, even on the cross streets. The neighborhood was settling in for the night, back doors opening and closing to let the cat out or to bring it in, depending on the temperament of the cat and of the owner.

Ian said it was time to leave. Lewis said it looked safe, but suggested that Ian leave the way he had come, and approach his parked car with caution. He left the security cameras on record and switched from the barber chair back to the walker.

Lewis turned off the motion detectors in the back yard so that the security lights wouldn't come on, then let Felonious out to check the fenced-in area. The big dog trotted around the perimeter of his domain, urinated in the far corner of the yard to mark what was his, and was back inside in five minutes.

Ian said, "I'll leave you my cell phone number. When this is over I'll take you to lunch at the oyster bar in the market."

"I'd like that. I don't get around much anymore."

Ian went out over the fence and back the way he had come.

He watched the street for a few minutes from another back yard, the one closest to his car. The house cat there came out to greet him, smelled Felonious on his clothes, and went back up onto the porch.

His car alarm was still set. The control panel showed that it hadn't been disturbed, that it hadn't gone off and reset itself while he was away from the vehicle. He drove past Lewis on the way out of the neighborhood, and got the all-clear on his cell phone a few minutes later.

Chapter 13
The Shadowed Owl

Ian's cell phone rang again as he drove back the way he had come. He was surprised to hear the the voice of the attorney, Irving Cordell.

"Ian Scott? This is Irving Cordell. We met at one of my fundraisers for the city bird project."

"Yes, I remember."

"Forgive the late hour, but I'm still in my office and I'd like to talk with you, if that's possible. Could you come by? Let me fix you a drink; I've got one of the best-stocked bars in the city. I have a business proposition that I know you'll find interesting."

"What kind of a proposition?"

"I'd rather not talk on the phone."

"Who else will be there?"

"Just the two of us, a private meeting. I'm right downtown; I'll give you the address. I can meet you in the lobby or you can have one of the security people come up to my office with you, if you prefer."

"It's almost midnight."

"I know it's late, but this is important."

"All right. I can be there in half an hour."

Ian had followed Ramsey when he left the downtown financial center, lost him on Queen Anne Hill, and now was going back downtown to have drinks with Ramsey's employer, the attorney Irving Cordell. A strange night. Had Ramsey spotted the surveillance and reported that to Cordell? Was this a trap?

Cordell seemed anxious to see him alone in the middle of the night. Did this mean that he didn't want Ramsey to know about the meeting? Had there been a falling out?

Why was Ramsey, the private eye, acting like a government spy? Who was he really working for? What was he doing? Ian's handling official still wanted answers.

Ian now knew that Ramsey had something to do with Adrian's disappearance, but was the attorney also involved? Maggie wanted answers, but most of all she wanted to know what had happened to her grandson.

Maggie and his handling official both had questions, but all he had were more questions. What little he did know about the two cases didn't make much sense. A late-night meeting with the attorney on his own turf didn't make much sense either, but handled properly, it would be safe enough.

Ian drove back downtown, this time to a nightclub with valet parking. He needed a place to leave his car off the street where someone could keep an eye on it. Ramsey might have still been prowling around.

Ian told the parking attendant at the club that he had a hot one lined up, and to keep the car within easy reach so that he and the girl could have a few drinks and leave in a hurry, before she cooled down. He said he knew the attendant would understand, and overpaid him to increase their understanding.

The parking attendant was a self-styled young man of the world who liked women who looked like the ones in porno films. He had seen several top-heavy young women enter the nightclub by themselves that night, but none that would be impressed with the way this guy was dressed. Image was everything in the clubs. This guy's outfit wasn't much, and he looked like he'd slept in it. It was a good thing he threw money around, because that was the only way he was going to get laid.

Ian overpaid the doorman as well, holding the bills in his fist with the corners showing as he approached the door so that the man could see the denominations and not turn him away for not fitting in with the club's image. Fisting the money hid the amount of the gratuity from onlookers, which worked to the doorman's advantage. Happy doormen act like old friends. He bumped fists with Ian, took the money, and waved him in.

Ian walked through the club as if looking for someone, then went to the men's room and sat in a stall for a couple of minutes, about the length of the average club patron's attention span at midnight. The place was filling up with flash and flair, and he wasn't noteworthy.

No one was looking his way when he came out of the men's room, so he left the club by the back door and walked the three blocks to the two-towers complex. The sidewalks were quiet except for the pools of activity near the clubs and restaurants that catered to the late-night crowd.

The attorney had given him the address of the North tower. As a precaution, Ian had one of the security people escort him up to Cordell's office. To protect himself, he wanted the guards to know where he was going and who he was meeting. Irving Cordell waved them into his office, then stood back to let them feel the full impact of their surroundings. The office was large, luxurious and impressive, as it was meant to be. The wine-colored wall-to-wall carpet was deep and expensive, something no amount of carpet padding could duplicate.

The office had been professionally decorated by someone who liked leather, with a large v-shaped desk, deep leather chairs and leather-topped side tables. The only things missing were the traditional shelves of leather-bound law books. Oil paintings of falcons in flight among the glass towers of the business district were a reflection of the attorney's involvement in the city bird project.

The young security guard who had escorted Ian up from the lobby was so impressed that he took his hat off. Ian thought the place looked more like a showroom than a working office. That was intentional, of course, but it made him feel even grubbier than he looked. So did the neatly dressed young security guard in a uniform that looked fresh from the cleaners.

Ian thanked the guard and let him leave.

Irving Cordell said, "Welcome, Mr. Scott. I'm so glad you could come on such short notice. Come in. Sit down and relax. May I fix you a drink? I'm having Southern Comfort, but you can have whatever you like. The bar is open."

He went over to the inside wall and slid back an oak panel. A light went on in the mirrored alcove behind the panel revealing a wet bar, a colorful display of liquor bottles from around the world, and a dazzling display of crystal. Ian knew this was also part of the carefully orchestrated display and decided to play along to help get things started.

He said, "Southern Comfort is fine."

Cordell brought Ian's drink and said, "Please call me Irving.

I want us to get to know each other. May I call you Ian?"

"If you like."

Cordell raised his glass. "Southern Comfort, a gentleman's drink. A nostalgic drink for the old spooks left over from the Cold War, and now the 'in' drink for the new generation of intelligencers. You've probably drunk Southern Comfort in a lot of strange places in your travels."

"I'm not sure what you mean."

"Let's stop beating around the bush, Ian. You're a former spook, and so am I. We were both underpaid and overworked, and have moved on to other things. I've been more successful in the private sector than you have, but that could change. Would you be interested in coming to work for me?"

"You're offering me a job?"

"I told you I had a business proposition."

Ian said, "I'm flattered by the offer. What exactly do you do?"

"I'm a competitor intelligence professional, one of the most successful. It's all about contacts, and no one has better contacts than I do. It's a good business, and you could be part of it."

Ian knew Irving Cordell was a spy, but that many spies in the private sector used competitor intelligence terms to describe themselves and their work. Ninety percent of the information they used was available from public records and other legitimate sources but the last, most important, ten percent was obtained by espionage. Clients paid well for that last ten percent, for obvious reasons. As they say, who wants only the first nine chapters of a ten-chapter book? Who would buy a book with the last chapter missing?

Cordell said, "Are you interested in my offer? I think we would make a good team. We have a lot in common."

Ian nodded. He wasn't going to argue with Cordell, at least not until he knew what the man had in mind. He was willing to subjugate his ego to gain information, to play dumb if necessary, something impossible for many people who live to blow their own horns.

Ian was dressed like a birder, and was grubby from his time on the roof of the financial center. He acted impressed by his present surroundings and kept smiling and nodding his head. The attorney knew better, but couldn't resist the temptation to talk the talk that went with his impressive office.

Cordell slid back another wall panel to reveal a high-tech computer center complete with all of the latest bells and whistles. The display included several pieces of German equipment, which always impressed Americans. Again, Ian thought it looked more like a showpiece than part of a working office.

The showpiece computer automatically went to the shadowed owl website of intelligence links. This seemed to imply that Cordell had government agencies access although most computers on the Internet could be set up to function that way.

Cordell said, "I use the latest computer equipment and subscribe to the best of the online data services. Most of my work is done by computer, but I need someone in the field to work with my contacts, someone to fill in the gaps while I do the rest."

Cordell was telling him a little about the legitimate side of his business, but Ian knew that. Like a crooked accountant, the attorney undoubtedly had more than one office and kept more than one set of books.

Ian said, "Don't you have someone already on staff to do the field work? A private investigator named Ramsey took one of my birding classes. I thought he worked for you."

"Ramsey worked for me for a while as a private contractor, but not any more. I fired him. I'm not looking for another private eye; I need someone with an intelligence background who could eventually become a partner. As I said before, we have a lot in common."

"In what way?"

"We both left government service under less than ideal conditions. I heard you had women problems. What did they do, give you crappy assignments until you quit?"

Ian said, "That was a long time ago. Old news, and not very interesting."

"I find it interesting. Newspaper databases are a valuable resource, especially the archives. Even the tattle sheets can be mined for information, though you have to know how to read between the lines. As I recall, the scandal involved a female embassy official who ran over your foot with a government car. What tabloid newspaper could pass up a story like that?"

"So what was your problem?"

"What do you mean?"

"You said we have a lot in common. Why did you leave government service?"

Cordell said, "They claimed I mishandled some government information. That was bullshit, of course. All I did was transfer some data to my laptop so that I could work on it away from the office. I put the laptop in the trunk of my car and forgot all about it until I went out to the parking lot the next morning. The laptop was still there, but the agency found out what I'd done. They accused me of purposely leaving the laptop where it could be accessed by an accomplice. They called it 'espionage by exposure'. That was bullshit too, of course. They chased their tails for a few months, but finally dropped the charges. You know how that goes."

Ian continued to sip his drink and nod as if he believed what Irving Cordell was saying.

He thought, yes, I know how that goes. Espionage by exposure is always difficult to prove, and I've heard these lies before.

Cordell directed the conversation away from himself by refilling their glasses with Southern Comfort and pointing to the computer alcove.

Cordell said, "Did you know that one of your papers on birding pretexts is still floating around on the Internet? I found it in the archives of one of the government websites. Look what you wrote on the subject."

Irving Cordell used voice recognition commands in French to bring the first page of Ian's white paper up on the big-screen monitor.

Ian had written, "I've watched birds and birders at sensitive locations in the U.S. and elsewhere, including along the Czechoslovakian border during the Cold War era. Birders are usually accepted as non-threatening friends of nature by local people, and are out at all hours of the day and night with their equipment adding to their lists of bird sounds and sightings.

"Modern spies purchase birding guides and monitor the local birding newsgroups on the Internet to learn more about the birds that fit their specific target areas. There are often a surprising number of birds to choose from. There are birds in cities, woodlands, waterways, and other locations worldwide. There are almost that many birding pretexts...Ian Scott— 16785."

"So, Ian, let's be frank with each other. You're not just an ordinary birder who's only interested in adding to his life list of sightings. Like me, you also have other interests. The same skills you used back then could make you a lot of money working with me in the private sector."

"Who would I actually be working for? Who are the clients?"

"I sell information on the open market."

"Even to people on the prohibited list?"

Irving Cordell said, "You know as well as I do that today's enemies are tomorrow's trading partners. The U.S. has done business with every enemy we've ever fought a war against, before and after the fact. I just get there first, ahead of the rest of the competition."

"You're talking about business espionage."

"In a sense, all espionage is business espionage. The government doesn't make weapons or any of the other things it needs in the basement of the Pentagon; it buys what it needs from companies in the private sector."

"You don't think there's anything wrong with what you're doing?"

"Right and wrong are religious concepts, like good and evil. They have nothing to do with the law, or with our profession. I've never been convicted of anything."

Ian didn't want to argue the point with Cordell, at least not now while the attorney was being expansive. He nodded his head and changed the subject.

"Why did you fire Ramsey? Is there something that I should know about? I don't want to walk into the middle of a feud, especially as I'd be the new guy."

"Ramsey didn't report in on time; he was unreliable. We had words and I let him go. That's all you need to know, at least for now."

Ian said, "Ramsey is a technical surveillance specialist, an eavesdropper, a spy. I know that for a fact because I've seen his work. That could come back to haunt you, since you were his employer."

Cordell looked shocked and pretended he didn't know anything about eavesdropping. When he didn't ask the usual what, where and when questions one would expect from an innocent party, it confirmed Ian's suspicions. Wouldn't an innocent person be asking questions? He knew Cordell was involved with at least some of Ramsey's electronic spying, and would probably now blame it all on the private eye.

Irving Cordell said, "I wouldn't put anything past Ramsey. I think he had something going on the side, but I don't know what. I didn't see it at first, and when I became suspicious and asked him about it, he became abusive."

"In what way? I need to know if I'm going to be a partner. I can handle just about anything that might come up, but I have to know what's going on."

Cordell thought, this guy must be tougher than he looks! He knows Ramsey but doesn't seem intimidated. Ramsey's a threat and it can only get worse. Maybe I can use this guy to get Ramsey off my back. I wonder what pushes Ian's buttons.

Cordell said, "Ramsey is an equal opportunity hater. He hates everyone who doesn't think the way he does. He especially hates two of the women he met in your birding class."

Ian suddenly looked up from his drink, an involuntary movement that betrayed his interest. He knew Ramsey hated May and Maggie, and May was dead.

Ian said, "Which women?"

"A young woman he had an argument with in your class, and an older woman who is bugging him about her grandson."

"He specifically mentioned an older woman with a missing grandson?"

"Yes. She's apparently been calling everyone from the utility companies to the agency that licenses private investigators

159

trying to track him down. He hasn't kept the P.I. agency informed of his whereabouts, so they called me looking for his new address."

"What did you tell them?"

"I told them what I know."

"That makes it a matter of public record, so now she knows as well."

Cordell thought, this guy is worried about the old lady! That's a button I can push.

Cordell said, "Ramsey has a violent streak. He hides it most of the time, but I hope the old lady has sense enough not to confront him by herself."

Ian put his glass down, still half full, and stood up. He looked grim. "Tell me everything you told the licensing people."

Cordell thought, my God, he's going after Ramsey! This guy either has brass balls, is a crazy son-of-a-bitch, or both. This couldn't be working out better! I hope he kills Ramsey, but if it's the other way around, Ramsey will end up in prison. I win either way.

Cordell said, "I'll tell you everything I know about Ramsey, but you better go armed. He never goes anywhere these days without a pistol."

Cordell provided an approximate address, the best information he had, but he didn't stop there. Ian was a weapon he was aiming at Ramsey, and he wanted to be sure that the weapon was fully loaded. He did everything he could to cast Ramsey in the worst possible light and to make him the scapegoat for any of their illegal activities that might come to light later. He talked for several minutes and in doing so he revealed more about his own involvement than he intended. It is hard to bad-mouth someone without revealing something about yourself.

Irving Cordell continued to volunteer information as they walked to the door of his office. He wanted to push as many of Ian's buttons as he could while he had the chance. He didn't stop talking until he closed the door behind him.

Cordell knew the building security guards had a record of Ian's visit. After Ian left he covered his ass by filling out a bogus employment interview form to show why Ian had been to the office. His notes on the interview form were carefully worded to make it appear that Ian had come to him with a questionable employment proposal, which he had rejected.

Chapter 14
Owl Pellets

It was now after midnight, a night of wind off the saltwater mixed with intermittent showers and the smell of rising damp. Typical Northwest weather. Ian picked up his car at the nightclub without incident and reported in by cell phone as he drove toward the industrial area along the slough south of the city. The area was sometimes referred to as "the slough of despond" by the local residents who had seen their quiet middle-class neighborhood change from one of modest well-kept homes to one of corroding aluminum storage sheds and the fenced-in equipment yards of industry. A few of the older residents stayed on despite rising taxes, mostly because of their memories of good times in the past.

Attorney Irving Cordell had supplied Ian with an approximate address for Ramsey, enough he hoped to track him down. Ramsey would probably have some sort of safe house in the depressed area near the slough.

Ian's handling official would want a record of what had

happened so far, especially if he found Ramsey and things went bad. Ian was required to produce two reports, one as a verbal stream of consciousness narrative recorded as close to the time of the incident being reported as possible, the other a standard written report produced later, in the calm after the storm. Sophisticated software would scan and compare the two accounts to merge the thoughts and images that were running through his mind at the time of the event, a form of psychological realism, with what he wrote later. Discrepancies between the two reports would be highlighted, but so would new insights. These analytical techniques produced a final work product that went far beyond the old-fashioned "just the facts" reports of previous generations of intelligencers.

Ian talked his stream of consciousness report into a special cell phone as he drove. The phone was supplied by his handling official and used only for these reports. As always, this phone was answered by a machine that asked, "What number are you calling?" What it really wanted was his I.D. number. Ian complied, heard a brief tone to indicate that his message was being recorded, and immediately began talking his report into the cell phone as he drove. He didn't know if someone was listening in as his talked, or how these reports were processed, but then they didn't think he needed to know.

James Joyce and Virginia Woolf wouldn't have thought much of his efforts. His stream of consciousness reports weren't masterpieces of introspection like Ulysses or Mrs. Dalloway, nor were they meant to be. They were less refined, less profound, less literary. They were more like the instinctive actions of an owl hunting at night, hanging in thin air on silent wings, then swooping down into the shadows, with no guarantee of success.

He didn't have all the parts of the puzzle, just bits and pieces. That was often the case early on. As a birder, he always thought of these early verbal reports, these fragments of information, as "owl pellets." Barn owls vomit up pellets of fur and bone after eating their prey. Researchers can sometimes reconstruct a skeleton from the fragmented remains found in an owl pellet, but they can only guess at the life and death struggle that produced it. Ian hoped the agency's analytical techniques could glean something useful from his own fragmented offerings.

He talked the report as he drove, letting the information flow unstructured. Some of the owl pellets came from Cordell, who had talked too much in an effort to distance himself from Ramsey, but most were based on his own feelings and impressions accumulated during the last three days.

Ian reported, "Meeting with attorney Irving Cordell, midnight, this date, North tower address you know. Cordell eager, anxious, alone, private meeting, security backup, frightened of Ramsey, fired probably, panic button under edge of desk, and hidden security cameras. Office setup, expensive, materialistic, overheated, strong scent of sandalwood, impressive, not working space. Hidden panel north wall, high-tech computer center, French voice recognition, some German equipment, mostly showpieces, automatically to website of shadowed owl intelligence links impression he has, more than one office and one set of books.

"Cordell suspects my birding class, 'Wildlife Surveillance with Camera & Recorder', is actually a cover, says he saw our ads online and in paper. I didn't argue. It has worked to our advantage so far. They keep coming out of the woodwork to Spy School, people of interest with links to other people of interest and so on who know how long it will continue to work. Let's keep running the ads.

"Cordell, probed with Southern Comfort, says we are both former spooks, underpaid, overworked, we both left service under a cloud, something we have in common. He's successful now in private sector offered me a job.

"Says he's a competitor intelligence professional, uses those terms to describe his work, says today's enemies are tomorrow's allies, get there first ahead of the competition. I'm reminded of early gem traders with people stationed in Africa on watch missions to help them dominate the gem market.

"Cordell says right and wrong and good and evil are only religious concepts, have nothing to do with the law. He was never convicted of anything. Says it's all about good contacts he finds through newspaper archives, tattle sheets and newsgroups on the Internet. I'm sure he's an industrial spy selling information from people, blackmailed, forced to cough up secrets, why else is he eavesdropping on private lives?

"Cordell says he was accused of mishandling government information, says bullshit, of course, transferred some data to laptop left in trunk of car overnight, I think espionage by exposure, he says charges were finally dropped. I've heard these lies before.

"Ramsey, private eye, acting like government spy, attorney, involvement for sure and more, lost him on Queen Anne Hill, strange night. He's a technical surveillance specialist eavesdropper, was/is planting and servicing bugs at and near financial center, also digiscoping private lives for personal secrets. I've seen his work, have sample tape. Has had one or more listening posts at the financial center on roof and at fools' phone, maybe probably also eavesdrops for his own amusement and/or to blackmail women for money and sex.

"Cordell fired, disavowed Ramsey, provided approximate address, nothing definite, he cast Ramsey in the worst possible light as scapegoat for illegal activities, my impression more lies Cordell's business built on old premise:

Intelligence gathering is like fishing
Hook a fish, you'll have fish for a day
Hook a fisherman, you'll have fish for
the life of the fisherman.

"Person with secrets targeted to produce other secrets, other breakthroughs when hooked. Dirty little secrets, anything derogatory put in private database checked, cross referenced, short-term, long-term patterns, developed information used against fisherman again and again to force spying.

"Irving Cordell, subtle modern-day spook, impression many financial clients, perhaps private bankers, financial consultants, front men for foreign governments, aren't they all one way or another, look at high-end brass plaque offices down quiet side streets near the parks overlooking the city, most cities. Clients want competitors's secrets and *intentions* of course re: funding recruiting investing facilities, inside information, not available outside inner circle at targeted firms.

"Cordell good at discovering derivative secrets and other spin-offs of information including some of my own real and planted. Probably does database searches using names of key people in targeted firms important suppliers, other contacts probed using several Internet identities, why not to support other identities in targeted pretext attacks. Internet searches to find key employees and contacts who give interviews, write articles, take part in research projects, targets are not aware of these leaks, all good sources. Derivative secrets, new human targets, confidential business relationships of special interest, all charted using H1 software to diagram the players since these relationships are not apparent until diagramed by computer. Birding is an executive pastime we should explore possibility. Cordell has been targeting executives in the birding groups and on worldwide birding tours using the methods just mentioned.

"Enterprise profile forms used to track targeted companies what spy didn't, then surveillance to identify specific human targets and chart their daily activities for surveillance setups at selected locations to gather inside info and relationships to other people of interest. Audio/video eavesdropping at offices and boardrooms and in intimate personal settings, my guess nothing about this technical surveillance goes into his reports to clients, he tells them he uses only public records and other open sources, this is a smokescreen to hide his illegal activities.

"Impression Irving Cordell tried to control P.I. Ramsey by keeping him, at least one remove didn't tell him the names of clients or why the assigned work was being done, probably wrote his own reports in the third person to mask the identities of operatives and informants he referred to only by his assigned numbers an old procedure but clients still like it, makes them feel safe. Digital photographs and other images are probably cropped to produce more material billable to clients double maybe triple billing, the results delivered direct or at drop sites by field men and other messengers, kept at least one remove he would maintain his own confidentiality at all costs.

"Overall impression of Irving Cordell, subtle, effective, takes minimal risks more to protect himself than his contacts, would use bugs, videotapes, wire taps, anything to beat his contacts into submission, doesn't trust anyone, probably keeps copies of his letters to his mother. I don't know her; perhaps he should.

"Impressions of P.I. Ramsey from my birding classes as previously reported and more, his conspiracy theories provide easy answers for life's complex problems, he needs easy answers a way to feel superior, a cause that gives him status, someone to sanction his violent actions, he thought the attorney supplied legal sanctions. Ramsey sees himself as a new-age high-tech spy, basically a loner but might join a group that supported the

167

violence, he likes it, goes armed, have seen him armed in the
park as previously reported.

"I know he's a killer,
"can't find him,
"can't prove it,
"I'm looking."

Chapter 15
Fly Away

Showers had turned to steady rain by the time Ian reached the small industrial area along the slough south of the city. He drove through the neighborhood the older residents called the "the slough of despond," a few modest well-kept old homes filled with the memories of good times long past, now surrounded by the ugly storage sheds and equipment yards that represented the future.

He was working alone. His owl pellets report had said nothing about his private involvement with Maggie Warren and her search for her grandson. What could he say? He had nothing concrete to report, and in any case, the search for Adrian was a private matter.

Attorney Irving Cordell had given an approximate address for Ramsey. Duane, the fat security guard at the financial center, had said Ramsey owned a castle on wheels. Ian took this to mean a recreational vehicle of some kind, one too large to fit in a standard garage.

He found the right place within a few minutes. The location made sense, at least for someone like Ramsey.

A small private home faced the street, but was partly hidden by lilac bushes. The house was dark. The driveway was empty. A storage shed sat at the back of the lot, a big metal building large enough to store an RV, or a boat and a trailer, or all three. It, too, was dark. A cheap red and white plastic "For Rent" sign had been taken down and leaned facing the side of the building. The words, in reverse, showed through the sign. Someone had been forced to rent part of their private space, another indication of neighborhood decline.

Ian parked next door in front of an equipment yard used by roofers. The smell of roofing tar was partially masked by the rain, but still pungent.

There were very few believable pretexts that worked in the rain in an industrial neighborhood after midnight. Even an owl prowl, or walking a dog, would be suspicious under the circumstances. Ian made do with what he had—a covered clipboard loaded with security survey checklists and a big black plastic flashlight favored by nightwatchmen. The same rumpled raincoat and hat he had worn earlier in the evening completed the improvised pretext. It was thin at best.

He walked openly along the front fence of the equipment yard, shining his flashlight as he went. He stopping to check the lock on the gate, then lifted the cover of the clipboard and wrote something inside. When he got to the corner of the fence closest to the building Ramsey was renting, he swept the beam of the flashlight down that side.

There were tire tracks in the mud where someone had backed a vehicle into the side of the metal building. A panel had given way and was pushed open far enough for a person to squeeze through.

Ian recognized the maneuver. Soldiers searching buildings under battlefield conditions sometimes crashed their vehicles through the sides of structures to bypass the alarms and booby-traps most often found near doorways. Police swat teams sometimes did the same.

Ian approached with caution. As he got closer, he saw that the tire tracks leading to the hole in the side of the building looked as if they'd been made by the special off-road tires on Maggie's Jeep. A broken piece of her license plate holder that read, "Mud buggy," confirmed it. *Maggie had gotten there first, and smashed her way in!*

What had she been thinking? These weren't the actions of a mild-mannered grandmother worried about her missing grandson. Had Maggie called Ramsey to ask about Adrian and been insulted, or worse yet, patronized? She was an old soldier not easily moved by insults, but Ramsey had called her "Adrian's little old granny" several times in birding class, and insults can fester.

For whatever reason, Maggie had rammed her way into the storage building, the actions of an angry person, and anger was debilitating. She'd be no match for a cold-blooded killer like Ramsey.

When no alarm went off, Maggie would have gone inside, perhaps without realizing that Ramsey might have a silent alarm with an automatic dialer that would call his cell phone if there was a break-in. As a spy, he wouldn't want to attract the attention of a burglar alarm company, or the police. He would want to handle intruders himself.

Maggie's Jeep was gone. Tire tracks led toward a back road to the property, so perhaps she had come and gone before Ramsey arrived. So where was Ramsey? Was he on his way, to arrive any minute, or already inside?

It was pitch black inside the building. Ian took a quick step to the side, stopped and listened, but heard only the rain far above on the metal roof. He had expected to find a recreational vehicle of some kind in use as a safe house, but the size of the RV parked inside the building took him by surprise. It was big enough for a safe house, with enough extra space for a workshop, perhaps in an extra bedroom. A bedroom-sized workspace with built-in benches and modular equipment racks can produce a surprising number of tiny eavesdropping devices in a relatively short time.

Ian walked around the RV. Everything was locked, with no sign of a break-in. It was probably alarmed, and perhaps booby-trapped. Maggie had apparently broken into the building, but not into the RV itself.

He knew that Ramsey would have installed his own burglar alarms, at least two systems, one for the building, and one for the RV. Since the RV hadn't been broken into, he looked for the building security system control box, hoping that the two were linked.

Ian found a control box hidden inside a metal storage locker bolted to the framework of the building. Ramsey had apparently assembled the alarm system himself using readily available components. As is often the case with do-it-yourself alarm projects, the electronics were fine; the weakest link was the thin metal housing of the control box itself. Ian warped the box out of shape by prying against it with a piece of scrap two-by-four until the lock let go and the door popped open.

He had hoped this was a master control for both alarm systems—the one for the building and the one for the RV. That wasn't the case. The box controlled only the components for the building system. The RV alarms and controls were out of reach inside the vehicle.

The building alarm system included wireless links to hidden security cameras, a video recorder, and a small monitor mounted inside the control box. When Ian punched the playback button on the video recorder, Maggie's face came up on the screen. Ramsey's voice on the security tape made him flinch.

Ramsey said, "You crazy old bitch! You couldn't leave it alone, could you? I'm tired of hearing your voice on my answering machine. Now you had to come looking, breaking into my place, poking your nose in my business. I'd shoot you right here if it didn't make such a mess."

The picture on the security tape was fuzzy, but clear enough to see that Ramsey was pointing a heavy revolver at Maggie. He motioned for her to raise her hands.

Maggie said, "What have you done with Adrian? I know you know something about his disappearance. He was always afraid of you. He told me so."

"Adrian was a thief. I heard he was trying to steal falcon chicks at the financial center, maybe he fell off a ledge."

Maggie said, "No one's reported finding his body."

Ramsey made an odd sound, something that might have passed for a laugh under different circumstances. He said, "Maybe he fell in a dumpster and got hauled away with the trash. Hell, he was a birder; maybe he just flew away!"

He waved Maggie toward the hole in the side of the building.

Ramsey said, "Now it's your turn to go. I know about your volunteer work with shorebirds; you talked about it in class. No one will question it when an old bird-watcher turns up missing while making her rounds out on the tide flats, especially late at night."

The security tape showed Ramsey and Maggie leaving the building. Ramsey had her by the coat collar from behind with the pistol against her back. His fist gripping her collar was wider than her neck.

The security tape continued to run for a few more seconds, stopped, then started again. Ian saw himself on the monitor beginning when the motion detectors had first sensed his presence as he entered the building.

He removed the security tape and took it with him.

He went outside. It was still raining. He followed the partially washed- out tracks of the Jeep toward some trees on the back road. One of Ramsey's nondescript older cars was parked off to the side, but Maggie's Jeep was gone.

There were signs of a violent struggle in the mud near where the Jeep had been parked. Blood had pooled in some of the footprints, now mixed with the rain. There were drag marks in the mud.

Ramsey wouldn't have wanted a crime scene at his safe house. Maggie must have forced the issue, tried to get away, and been killed on the spot.

Chapter 16
Bowerman Basin

Ian drove to Bowerman Basin, a saltwater haven for migratory shorebirds on the Pacific Flyway. He called in another report to his handling official as he drove, straight talk this time, a short report, just the facts. He wanted someone to know where he was going, and why, in case he didn't come back. He said only that he was still hunting Ramsey, with no success.

He left out what he had seen on the security tape in Ramsey's safe house, and in the mud near where Maggie's Jeep had been parked. He didn't want the agency or the local police involved, at least not yet. It wasn't that he didn't trust the system to do the right thing; it was just that it took so long to do it. It is called the criminal justice system, not the victim's justice system, for obvious reasons.

Maggie was a volunteer with a shorebird project, something to do with bird counts at night on the tide flats. According to the security tape at Ramsey's safe house, Ramsey planned to get rid of Maggie near her work site. It was a good place to get rid of a body, a place that was far from his safe house and had no connection with him.

Ian arrived at Bowerman Basin in the darkness before dawn. It had been a long, tense drive in the rain that never let up. He was tired and his ankle was sore. He had loosened his laces, but it didn't help. He rolled down his window to get his bearings and to look for the dirt road that led to the tidal area. An unseen flock of shorebirds moved across the night sky in the distance. Their cries were muted by the rain.

Maggie's Jeep was parked above the high-tide line in an area that opened directly onto the tide flats. There was no one in sight as he drove by. He stopped, turned off his lights and tried the night scope, but it was useless because of the rain.

He parked on the other side of a pile of driftwood. It wasn't enough to hide his car, but he hoped it was enough to break up its silhouette. The driftwood smelled of dried seaweed and barnacles, the smell of iodine mixed with old bones.

Ian got out of his car and walked back toward the Jeep. He carried a flashlight and a revolver. He pulled the hand that held the flashlight up into the sleeve of his raincoat to dim the light, a poacher's trick that left his gun hand free.

The rain had increased. His pants legs below the raincoat soon soaked through and clung to his legs.

He could see the outline of the Jeep, but little of what lay beyond. The Jeep was locked. There were drag marks in the mud leading out on the tide flats, a broad smooth trail. Something was being pulled toward the water on a tarp, or a rug, or a piece of canvas. He followed the trail through the mud.

He hadn't gone more than ten yards when the mud sucked his shoes off his feet. To retrieve them he would have to juggle the flashlight and the revolver, pull the shoes out of the mud, and try to put them back on while standing on one foot. The risk was too great. He left his shoes where they were and walked on without them.

To walk barefoot through the mud of tide flats was to walk back in time, the ooze a reminder of who we are, and where we came from. The mud was home to small creatures low on the food chain but vital to life on our planet. Ian could feel them moving beneath his feet as he followed the drag trail toward the water.

When he got close enough to hear the sounds of the drag, he steadied his gun hand across the arm that held the flashlight and pointed the beam in that direction. When he saw who it was, he lowered the pistol.

Maggie was the one dragging the tarp toward the water!

She jumped back, exhausted but defiant.

Ian kept the revolver in his right hand and opened the tarp with the hand that held the light. Ramsey was staring back at him, dead, with his head split open.

Maggie's entrenching tool was laying on top of the body. The handle was covered with blood. In use since WWI, the entrenching tool has always been the soldier's friend, outlasting other tools of the trade, including the bayonet.

Ian thought, Ramsey saw a little old lady, not a tough old soldier with a razor-sharp weapon.

Ian said, "I saw your tire tracks in the alley at Ramsey's place. What happened?"

Maggie was breathing hard from dragging the body.

She said, "Ramsey caught me at his safe house. The bastard just grinned at me when I asked about Adrian. He didn't want a crime scene near his place so he told me to get in the jeep. He was still grinning that shitty grin of his and calling me "Adrian's Granny" as I climbed in. I grabbed my entrenching tool from between the seats and whacked him."

Ian said, "He weighs twice what you do. How did you get him into the Jeep?"

"I moved the Jeep over under a tree, put the top down, threw the winch cable over a tree branch, and winched him in. Then I put the top back up, and drove out here to the mud flats."

"You should have left this to me. You could have been killed!"

"I know how to deal with trash like this. I take care of my own."

Ian said, "You've done this before?"

He knew that Maggie had lost a son to drugs supplied by a drug dealer who disappeared farther down the coast, near the beach at Moon Bay. The police there had never been able to locate the dealer. Ian had thought at the time that Maggie might know something about the man's disappearance, since she hadn't pursued the matter. Her silence now confirmed his suspicions.

Ian put the pistol back in his raincoat pocket and handed the flashlight to Maggie. She put her hat over the end to dim the light. Ian closed Ramsey's eyes and folded his arms across his chest.

He took a deep breath of the clean salt air coming in with the tide, wiped the handle of the entrenching tool on the dead man's jacket, and began to dig a grave in the mud next to the body. As he dug he could feel the mud oozing between his bare toes.

Each turn of the tide would fill in and smooth out the gravesite as the body settled and became part of the food chain. The tide is a good provider. It had almost reached the grave as he finished burying the body.

Ian said, "You've got to stop killing people. You aren't some medieval Mason who has taken an oath to bury evildoers at the low-tide mark."

Maggie said, "He killed Adrian, my only grandchild."

"I know, but you've got to stop killing people." *

"I will, if they will."

Epilogue

Adrian's body was found by a woman on the housekeeping staff at the financial center. He had fallen from the fourteenth floor to the tenth and died when his head hit the side of the building. His body came to rest face down on the decorative ledge above one of the windows. As the muscles of his body relaxed in the days that followed, his arm swung down in front of the window where it was caught by the wind. The cleaning woman looked up from her work, saw the dead arm wave to her, crossed herself, and fainted for the first time in her life.

Maggie buried her grandson next to her son near Moon Bay. When the shorebird research project at Bowerman Basin concluded, she moved back to Moon Bay to be near their graves.

Ramsey's body was never found.

Attorney Irving Cordell continued to be successful as a competitor intelligence agent. Economic espionage was a growth industry, by whatever name. The government eventually brought charges against him for espionage, but was unable to prove its case.

Buster, the little dog, was out of the spy business and found a new career with a young family down a quiet side street in the city. He checked his p-mail on walks with the family and participated in a game called "trying to run over Buster" that included a small girl on a tricycle.

Ian Scott continued teaching birding classes and housesitting for friends and other birds of passage. He kept in touch with Laura Cole, who finished her work on the new exhibit at the zoo and went back to the England. Timing was everything in romantic relationships, as it was in so much of life.

The timing was wrong for them at the zoo, but perhaps in England in April, after the Bewick's swans leave Slimbridge on migration to their breeding grounds in Russia...

Printed in the United States
38992LVS00002B/187-204